Buffalo Spring

Also by Fred Grove
in Large Print:

Bitter Trumpet
The Buffalo Runners
Comanche Captives
Deception Trail
A Distance of Ground
The Great Horse Race
Into the Far Mountains
Man on a Red Horse
Match Race
Phantom Warrior
Search for the Breed
Trail Rogues

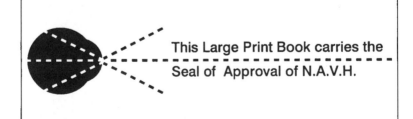

This Large Print Book carries the
Seal of Approval of N.A.V.H.

Buffalo Spring

Fred Grove

Thorndike Press • Waterville, Maine

Published in 2002 by arrangement with Golden West Literary Agency.

Thorndike Press Large Print Western Series.

The tree indicium is a trademark of Thorndike Press.

The text of this Large Print edition is unabridged.
Other aspects of the book may vary from the original edition.

Set in 16 pt. Plantin by Christina S. Huff.

Printed in the United States on permanent paper.

Library of Congress Cataloging-in-Publication Data

Grove, Fred.
    Buffalo spring / Fred Grove.
        p.   cm.
    ISBN 0-7862-3985-9 (lg. print : hc : alk. paper)
    1. American bison hunting — Fiction.   2. Large type books.
I. Title.
PS3557.R7 B85 2002
813´.54—dc21   2001054083

Buffalo Spring

Chapter 1

Martin Roebuck, stretching himself by the wagon, inhaled deeply and watched pale light dapple the eastern sky. Grass smell rolled in on the southwestern wind, bringing an impression of unending space, spilling images of the lush prairies, wooded hills, and running creeks of the north Texas buffalo country. He stood still, all his being at ease, and the darkness changed ever so subtly again, flushing a rose dawn, revealing the rounded blur of the Army ambulance in which the young woman rode and slept.

A low shape seemed to materialize out of the ground at Martin's feet. "Tack," he said. The dog nosed Martin's hand, licking, whining softly; in turn Martin rubbed the broad head and stroked the thick ruff. Each morning it was the same, almost ceremonial. The massive mongrel appearing, as silent as smoke, ready with his faithful greeting. A source of pleasure, that trust, and also strange, for Tack had savage blood. A trust, Martin reflected, of which few men, even old friends, were worthy.

For another interval man and dog stood

close together, peering off into the murk. A deeper hue pinked the dimness. The illusion of harmony between earth and sky lingered until a trooper in the mail escort rose grumbling and stomped into his boots.

After breakfast, Lieutenant William Egan strode across. "Going off trail this morning," he said apologetically. "Want to swing around a stretch south of the Pease where the Indians like to jump small detachments like ours. I regret the delay."

Egan's sunburned, unshaven face suggested that of an older officer. He impressed Martin as conscientious and efficient, but no hewer to the book.

"Never mind that, Lieutenant," Martin said. "You're letting us tag along. We camped two days at Doan's Crossing, waiting for you."

Egan's formality gave way to frankness. "I'm not so altruistic as you think. Your outfit means two more rifles. And besides the Fort Griffin mail, we've got a passenger." His eyebrows went up. "Or have you noticed?"

"I have. Looks like interesting duty."

"Her father," Egan said, impressed, "is Fielding Sanford."

"Sanford — the naturalist?"

"Dr. Fielding Sanford. None other. Went

8

before the Texas legislature . . . tried to get a law passed to save the buffalo. They laughed at him. He must have high government connections. Otherwise, the Army wouldn't be furnishing her transportation. She's on her way to meet him." Egan turned. "I dare say your noble dog there could escort the lot of us through without difficulty."

Tack lay under the wagon, as indolent as a young lion, and as regal, his shaggy tan head resting between stubby paws, his large brown eyes calmly observant, his alert ears, twitching to the changing camp sounds, as upright as guidon staffs. In all, he presented a curious mixture of colors, from the handsome silver ruff and the pumpkin-colored brows to the powerful black body flecked with gray, corroborative of strength and endurance. Martin had fashioned a collar for him from a leather strap and harness buckle and the buckle shone.

A little game was being played between Tack and Augustin, the undersized Frenchman who drove the team and cooked. He held up a skillet at the dog, which rose at once, and struck tantalizing taps on the iron with a spoon, teasing. "You don' eat lak dog. *Non.* You eat lak human. *Oui.* Maybe so Tack is human — *oui?*" And he poured a lake of gravy, leftover biscuits, and hunks of meat into an enormous pan.

Egan, still admiring, asked, "Mind telling me where you got him?"

Martin had told how at nearly every settlement since leaving the Cherokee Nation. "It's a long story," he said.

"Later then," Egan said, gauging the morning sun.

Throughout the early morning Martin rode alongside the wagon, trailing the Army ambulance. Tack took his customary position to the rear; now and then he would roam to either side, to scout out a mesquite thicket or to pause, rock-still, and sniff the grass-scented wind.

True, there was a monotony about this country as it dipped and rolled toward the Clear Fork Valley of the Brazos, about three days' journey south. But Martin did not find it wearisome. As the sun mounted higher in the cloudless blue sky, bluer than in Missouri, it struck the early spring buffalo grass and distorted remote objects. Once he thought he saw a shimmering lake; when he looked again, it had vanished, only a flickering mirage. White heat hazed the infinite distance and the eternal wind pulled at his face and clothing, though not unpleasantly.

He became conscious of a lulling effect, of a release of the spirit. What his eyes found in the sweeping distance seemed to free him inside, letting the mind drift, leaving him alternately soothed and lifted up. It helped him put aside for the time his reason for coming so far to return to the frontier.

This boundless country had a silence, too, a wrongness and emptiness, which puzzled and nagged him. When the little column halted around ten o'clock, he rode up to Lieutenant Egan and asked, "Where's the buffalo?"

Egan's slim face turned thoughtful. "Shot out, sir. Been that way through here for two years . . . since '77. Main hunting's all west and northwest of Griffin now."

"Hard to believe," Martin said, thinking of Kansas.

"Not when more than a hundred thousand hides were hauled out of Griffin last fall and winter. Maybe two hundred thousand. You'll see as we get closer to the Clear Fork range. Maybe later today."

"You mean — ?"

"Bones — you'll see bones, sir. The hunters are doing the Army's job, actually. By killing off the buffalo, they've just about put the Indian on the reservation. Something the Army couldn't do."

Ahead the glazy land ruffled up and the escort, winding around for the benefit of the vehicles, descended a gentle slope and filed toward a timbered branch.

Tack, muzzle high, sniffing the breeze, sprang ahead into a clump of post oaks. The escort trotted on, turning parallel to the branch. Egan, in advance, reined short and threw up his halting hand, passing a command as he did so, and the troopers drew carbines and fanned out.

Martin halted in surprise at sight of the tipi. A single hide lodge facing east, the door flap flung back, the lower part of the tipi raised for coolness. Nothing moved.

Tack faced the doorway, hair bristling, growling, motionless. Martin rode over just as Egan did.

"Something's in there," Egan said, getting down.

Martin dismounted, called the dog back, drew his revolver and looked inside. Light streaming through the tipi's smoke vent showed the fire-pit's dead ashes. Somewhere the wind flapped a loose hide. Martin smelled the old skins covering the cedar poles. Toward the rear he could see a reclining shape, beside it an open skin bag and a hollow gourd.

A chill touched him as he ducked inside and gazed down at the small figure in the buckskin dress drawn up on the buffalo robe. Egan tramped in behind him. The skin bag, apparently used to store meat, and the gourd were empty; and now the close smell of the lodge reached Martin as stale mesquite smoke and dust.

"An old woman," Egan observed. "She hasn't been dead very long."

Martin was watching the wizened features in revulsion. At the sound of Egan's voice a clawlike hand fluttered up, and Martin flinched. He stepped back and suddenly, quite suddenly, he was staring into beady, coffee-colored eyes.

"By God" — Egan jerked — "she's alive!"

They kept staring at her, uncertain what to do, while the strange eyes, as if just now understanding these were white men, grew larger with fright.

"She's afraid of us," Martin said, "and no wonder." He holstered his weapon and faced Egan; together they turned and stepped outside.

"I've heard of this," Egan said, gazing around the tipi. "Indians leaving their old people to die when they get helpless."

"A cruel custom, I'd say."

"To us, yes, though it's not lack of affection. Notice how they dressed her up? Nice buckskins, beads. Good moccasins. Left her food and water."

"I can't see that," Martin differed.

"It's partly necessity when the old ones can't travel, and also fear of the evil spirits. The dying person's ghost." Egan made a small, wry grimace. "Looks like the old girl fooled 'em."

"I wonder if her people will come back?"

"Not a chance. Too superstitious."

"Well," Martin said, "we just can't ride off and leave her. She'll die here without food and water."

A thought formed in his mind and he saw it shape likewise in Egan's face. Of one accord, they re-entered the smelly lodge. Besides the buffalo robe, she lay on a sort of willow mat. When they took the ends and lifted, her eyes pushed out and she gripped the mat's sides and shrilled her fierce, unintelligible wrath at them. And when they put her down outside, and by now the curious troopers had gathered, she voiced her defiance again.

"She's not as weak as I thought," Martin said and called for Augustin to bring brandy.

He came waving a brown, round bottle. As Martin knelt beside her and pulled the cork, she divined his purpose and her smoky eyes flashed. He trickled several drops between her cracked lips. Blinking, puckering her distaste, she spat the fiery liquid back at him.

Egan, smothering a grin, dispatched a cavalryman after the gourd to fetch water from the branch. When she saw the water, she rolled over on her side and drank in long gulps, pressing veined hands to the dipper; and when Augustin brought cold biscuits and meat, she wolfed every crumb, every shred.

"She no eat long time," Augustin said.

Afterward, she lay back, strengthless, and leveled her hostility on Martin.

Egan smiled. "Don't believe she cottons to your brandy, Mr. Roebuck."

"Nor to white men," Martin agreed. "Could be, Indian-like, she's mad because she wanted to die and here we come along."

No matter, he could not deny her his sympathy. She looked pathetically ancient and wasted. Her eroded face, as wiveled as a prune's skin, reminded him of a medieval witch, her cropped gray hair of wisps of thin, dry grass. Her teeth were worn to brown stubs. Only her eyes held vitality. In them he saw unquenchable life still and simmering hate for the blue pony soldiers around him, and for himself as well.

"What tribe is she?" Martin asked aloud and realized he was merely delaying something.

"Comanch'," vouched an old trooper.

"How can you tell?"

"Them fringes on her moccasins. Them jinglers. She's Comanch', all right. Seen many a one at Fort Sill."

Everyone stood around in silent dismay. The old Indian woman raised up, her dark eyes sensing and wondering, flicking from white man to white man. Her fear wasn't so evident now, though Martin could see it behind her primitive watchfulness. She wasn't begging either. As visible as if she shouted in English, her time-scoured face seemed to say: *You gave me food and water. But I do not trust you. You are white men. So kill me. I am Comanche!*

Pity fell upon Martin, and a stirring of respect, for he saw that she was a brave old person.

It was Egan who broke the unresolved quiet. "Now what?" he said, as much to himself, and rubbed the back of his neck.

"We can put her in my wagon —"

What was Martin saying? He had spoken spontaneously, not thinking, and the first reaction he saw was that of Augustin, whose mouth hinged down to frame a solemn objection.

"We can take her to the town of Griffin, can't we?" Martin asked, and as he spoke it occurred to him that, instead, he was seeking to convince himself. "Isn't there a

16

doctor there?" he went on. "I understand Indians live near the fort. Won't they look after one of their own kind?" No one answered. He felt a start of impatience, of partial anger. "Somebody give me a hand," he said.

He wasn't expecting the rustle of skirts behind him. Nor the calm voice saying, "Let me help her." He turned. Miss Sanford brushed past him, knelt beside the Indian woman and touched her shoulder to reassure her. The old Comanche looked too weak to object.

Martin started toward them. Miss Sanford's voice stopped him: "I can help her walk. Just lift her into the wagon."

She was looking up at him, and in that moment he saw her face up close for the first time. The hazel eyes, full of concern. Her hair reddish brown in the sunlight, in curls beneath the absurdly small hat and its incongruous cluster of imitation pink rose buds.

Moments later he hesitated by the wagon, revealing his repugnance at handling the smelly figure, and Miss Sanford's clear voice came:

"She won't bite. She's not strong enough."

Martin's face burned. Egan and the troopers watched, too, in amusement. So then he picked up the old woman and set

17

her inside as easily as he would a small child.

The escort was in motion when Egan rode back and said, "I didn't say anything back there. Not the way your mind was set. But the Indians at Griffin are Tonkawas. Tonks and Comanches are hereditary enemies. They kill each other on sight."

One corner of Martin's mouth curled upward in a faint smile. "That the only reason you didn't speak up, Lieutenant?"

Later in the morning Martin's horse shied and he saw the first bleached rubble of bones and the curved-horn skull of a buffalo, white upon the undulating sea of curly short grass. Onward, still more bones, an entire prairie of loose bones, scattered by wolves, endless until a hill broke the littered pattern.

Martin's mind reached back and suddenly he remembered — a stand. Some hunter had a stand here. Only once had he experienced such a run of wanton shooting. Sid Trumbo was with him that still, hot afternoon. He could see the buffalo again, sluggish after drinking their fill of creek water and weary after being bombarded from another watering place. The wind just right, from the buffalo to him. Shooting only the outside animals, until almost a hundred lay scattered about, and he had quit, too sickened to kill any more.

Necessity was forcing Egan to take the escort directly across the wide, littered plain. Bones clanked and crunched under the iron wagon rims, causing the temperish mules to step gingerly. Nothing so much as stirred across the glittering distance. In all directions the country was quite lifeless, and a thoughtfulness settled over Martin. He was glad when the column swung back to the broad cattle trail.

That afternoon a fog of dust rose to the south, and Martin began to see riders and hear cattle bawling. Egan turned off to let the longhorns pass on north.

Not long afterward, a small trail seemed to sneak in from the west to join the broader one, and there beside the road fork, pointing south, Martin found this sign on a pole:

R. H. HILLYARD
FORT GRIFFIN

—

HIDES — BONES
TOP PRICES

At bivouac after the mules were unhitched, watered and fed, Martin saw the question clouding the Frenchman's face and delaying his cooking.

"What we do 'bout the old one, huh?"

Augustin demanded, fixing hands on hips.

"Put up the other shelter tent."

"*Mon Dieu,* our new tent? That old woman, she stinks. *Non!* I, Augustin Girard" — he beat his knuckles upon his banty-rooster chest and arched back his head — "am no nurse. I am a man. I quit!"

"She won't be with us long. Just to Griffin."

"*Non!*"

"You won't have to feed her. I'll do that."

About once a week, ever since leaving St. Louis, the irascible little Frenchman's temper let fly and he threatened to quit over reasons either real or fancied. Black-haired, black-eyed, unwell, he could summon a choleric excitability in a twinkling. Just as swiftly it would recede, leaving a penitent middle-aged man who next, as impulsively, couldn't do enough for you. Thus, Martin had learned to wait him out.

Augustin's stormy gaze shifted from Martin to the dog and dwelled there without change of expression. A long moment and Augustin, shuffling, turned his head from side to side. When he looked up, Martin saw the usual, undeniable repentance amending the sharp features. The flexible, moody mouth knitted, the pendulous lower lip protruded. One bony shoulder rose and fell. The ingratiating black eyes beseeched, "Maybe so Augustus fix supper pretty damn quick, huh?"

Almost smiling, Martin stepped to the rear of the wagon. The old woman lay on one of his blankets. She seemed aware of his presence at the same time, as if some aboriginal sense told her, and she sat up and the smoky eyes, frightened again, beheld him in alarm: *You are a white man. When are you going to kill me?*

In exasperation, he made signs for eating and drinking. Little by little her fear lessened and she nodded, understanding, and the wilted face even parted in a wrinkled grin which exposed the nubby teeth.

Augustin looked in on his way for firewood. As he did, the Comanche woman pointed outside. Martin was puzzled. She pointed again the same way, faster, and, more slowly, to herself and outside, an unmistakable gesture.

Martin's face flashed hot. He met the squeamish, yet devilish, eye of Augustin, who shrugged and hurried on, murmuring, "Augustin, he fix tent."

And the old woman laughed for the first time, a cackling laugh, which said she was enjoying the distress of two despised white men.

She felt no heavier than a light blanket as Martin helped her, hobbling, to the mesquite thicket. There, violently, she motioned him away. Minutes passed before he thought of her again, and when he glanced across, she was dragging herself along the ground toward camp.

A pang of conscience smote Martin. He strode out to her.

Contempt and scorn for him, a mere white man, heightened across her sun-wrinkled face. That was when he noticed how straight and strong and proud her nose was, its prow almost touching her cupped-up chin. She signed for him to go. He started to and changed his mind, annoyed by her perversity. And so he lifted her to her feet.

She eyed the little shelter tent in pleased surprise and motioned Martin to let her sit in the doorway. Seated on the grass, she craned her head to inspect the walls, the short pole and the peak just over her head, meanwhile sniffing the strange canvas smells like a wild animal.

Tack approached, as curious of her as she was the tent. Martin called him back. Soon after, when he looked again, she was stroking Tack's ruff and their heads were almost touching as she talked to him in low tones. Martin scowled. He could swear that Tack seemed to understand her.

At supper she wolfed the generous helpings, eating with her fingers and wiping them on her buckskin dress. And Augustin, not Martin, took her a second plateful and returned marveling.

"She no eat long, long time," he said.

"From the looks of that old tipi," Martin reflected, "her people didn't leave her much food, figuring she'd die soon, anyway. Or could be they didn't have much to leave."

A freshening wind sprang out of the southwest, cool on the face and whimpering in the ear. The last of the blood-red sun lay glowing in scarlet beyond yonder side of a long-running ridge. Camp sounds diminished to the murmur of troopers' tired voices and the steady grass-cropping of picketed mules and cavalry mounts. Tack left the wagon to prowl the shadows purpling the spring. In the filmy twilight Martin could imagine the old Indian woman in her tent, as alert as a wolf to the night's early stirrings, longing for the people who had abandoned her, black eyes upturned to the close walls of the white man which enclosed her.

Before dark Martin saw Miss Sanford, hatless, walking gracefully across from her wagon. Remembering her display of sympathy for the old Comanche, he realized he had expected to see her during the evening. He came to his feet.

"I'm Harriet Sanford."

"Martin Roebuck."

"How is the Indian lady?"

"Lady?" He had to restrain a low laugh.

"I'm sure you could call her that among her own people," she said in a cultivated voice that was quite differing, yet thoroughly charming to the ear.

"Such a thought just never occurred to me," he replied, tempering the remark. "She did eat a good supper."

The coolness between them thawed a little. She was, he decided, not so tall as he had first supposed because of her straight carriage. And she was slender rather than thin, and small rather than slight, and her mouth was even and full and sensitive. Without her hat he saw that she wore her hair in curls that lay well back; smaller brown curls clung over her high forehead. He found himself wishing to please her.

"Maybe she'll be all right in a few days," he said.

"I hope so. I have the feeling it is mainly a lack of proper nutrition."

"Nutrition?" He grinned over that one. "She's eighty-five if she's a day."

Her small chin lifted until she looked into his eyes. "What I mean, Mr. Roebuck, is that with the bison being slaughtered, many of the Plains tribes in the Southwest — Comanches, Kiowas, Cheyennes — are starving. When I came through Fort Sill, one Comanche band had just surrendered. You should have seen how terrible they looked, especially the children. All eyes. But they weren't crying." He was silent before her intensity. She said: "I thought of those hungry children today as we passed through that great field of buffalo bones."

He was beginning to feel uncomfortable. "Would you like to see our friend?" he suggested.

"Indeed. Even though we can't understand each other."

Martin accompanied her to the shelter tent and left. Glancing back later, he saw the two women sitting across from each other, and he experienced the odd perception that, despite their silence, a vague communion existed between them.

Harriet Sanford had gone when Lieutenant Egan tramped in from inspecting the sentry posts. He accepted a cup of coffee, sat on a box and cocked his head in the direction of the tent. "How's our captive?"

"Give her two more days and she'll be taking over your command," Martin predicted. "I've been doing some thinking, Lieutenant. Why can't the Army provide her transportation from Fort Griffin to Fort Sill, near the Comanche reservation?"

"Could — if. If we secured permission from all concerned — Washington, for one. The Society of Friends, for another, which manages Comanche affairs. And the post commanders at Griffin and Sill. Let's see . . . that shouldn't take over six months." Egan's voice scattered a light ridicule which Martin did not find entertaining.

"Simpler," he said, "just to put her in an Army wagon and deliver her back to her people."

"Now you're making things too simple, at least for the Army."

"Wouldn't it?"

"It would. But how do we know her people are there? They just left her to die a few days ago. If they're not on the reservation — and I have an idea they're out hunting for buffalo — she'd refuse to go."

"Oh, come now, Lieutenant. She's hardly in a position to refuse." By this time, Martin saw, the old woman's disposition had become a game of banter between them. He said, "I am deeply moved by the Army's tender solicitude for the whims of an Indian crone so savage and brimming with hate."

"Can you blame her?" Egan answered, projecting a surprising sympathy. "Look how the white man is cleaning out his red brother's commissary."

"You don't mean that. Wiping out the buffalo? That's impossible."

Egan held the tin cup on his knee, not speaking for several moments. "Let me tell you that three years ago from Griffin to the Pease was black with Buffalo this time of year. We had to halt the wagons again and again to let the big shaggies pass. Quite a sight. Something I haven't seen since and likely won't again. So far we haven't spotted a single buffalo, and we won't."

"Still hard to believe," Martin said, frowning at Egan's finality. "And let me tell you that after we reach Griffin I can't haul that old woman on out to buffalo country."

"I'll talk to the post commander." Egan was being purposely vague again. He finished his coffee and rose to go. "Now, where'd you get that dog?"

"Coming out. In Indian Territory. Cherokee country."

"So he's an Indian dog?"

"Don't know. Could've come from a white settlement."

"And grew up wild," Egan conjectured.

"All I know is he turned up one morning. I looked back and there he was, gaunt and wild, following like an old stock dog. Didn't

27

look wolf enough to shoot."

"Maybe it was the orange eyebrows," Egan laughed.

"That — and the way he acted. Like he wanted to make friends, but didn't know how. All that day he followed us, and the next, keeping the same distance. About ten rods . . . I started leaving him food of an evening. He'd take it off, disappear, come back . . . Wouldn't let us come near him. At night he'd be where he could watch camp. Never barked. Never bothered the mules. That went on four or five days. Till one morning. I got up and there he was, waiting. Come to camp."

"Must weigh a hundred pounds," Egan guessed.

"One-twenty is closer."

"I suppose he fights wolves?"

"On the contrary, I think he goes out at night and plays with 'em."

"What would you say his breeding is?"

It was Martin's turn to show amusement. "You've got me there. Wolf and shepherd, I guess."

"*Non*," Augustin broke in. "Tack, he is ver' human."

On the third day after leaving Doan's Crossing on Red River, Martin Roebuck saw the wooded hills and ridges jostling and

rising, and before long the escort filed down
to the Clear Fork of the Brazos, shrunk to
low, glistening pools. And there by the
crossing reared another R. H. Hillyard sign,
reading the same as the one seen earlier up
the cattle trail.

A distant drone reached Martin, an intru-
sion upon the quiet afternoon. He wasn't
prepared for the boisterous settlement
teeming across the river, below the fort on
the rocky hill where the flag flew. Enough
tents and wagons for an Army crowding the
wide flat between village and river and
spreading downvalley. Long, high embank-
ments darkening the landscape. Hide yards.
Acres of hides. Like Dodge, he thought.

Egan held up on the other side of the
stream for the column to close up, and
Martin, riding forward, reminded him, "Remember, if I don't hear from you tomorrow,
I'm going to make the fort a present of one
very old and very smelly Indian woman."

With a wave, Egan took his troopers along
the road. The Army ambulance followed.
Harriet Sanford rode beside the driver.

"How long will you be here?" she called.

"Day or two."

"Where will you camp?" She was looking
back at him as she asked.

He flung up his hand. "Downriver, I guess."

29

Watching the ambulance go on, he wondered whether he would see her again. A reminding stink fouled the warm wind, stink from the hide yards and the numerous camps, and after looking over the crowded flat, he turned down the valley. Half a mile farther he found clean open ground among mesquites not far from the river.

While Augustin went for water, Martin put up the shelter tent and turned to help the Comanche woman out of the wagon. He stopped short.

She was holding to a rear wagon wheel, her lined face pointed questioningly to the hum of the raucous settlement. Martin stepped nearer. She turned and, although she no longer showed fear of him, he saw her distrust and perplexity. The black eyes asked. *What are you going to do?*

He extended his right hand toward her. Her eyes lifted from it to his face, a rejecting expression. She ignored him and set out the short distance for the tent, hobbling, and sank down in the little doorway, spent, and raised her worn face to the brilliant sunlight, as if she sought strength from it.

Watching her, he realized that after three days his misgivings of her as a burden had altered. She did not complain. She ate the white man's strange food in dignified gratitude, never humbly. It amazed him, in truth, how little trouble she was.

Augustin returned from the river and Martin said, "The old woman walked all the way to her tent."

"*Grand-mère,* she is much stronger." Augustin was elated. "Pretty soon she go home, huh?"

An old question by now. Martin spread his hands in imitation of Augustin and shrugged. Soon afterward he was riding toward the noisy town.

Sid Trumbo filled his mind. What was he like now? How much had he changed? The money seemed almost secondary.

At the first stinking hide yard, Martin saw another R. H. Hillyard sign, with one additional note: NO TRESPASSING. Before him the settlement took brash, outflung shape, its boisterous voice rising and falling over its tangle of adobe and picket houses, corrals and store buildings. Main Street, which extended from the base of the stony bluff to the river, was two rows of high-faced frame structures which appeared to glower at one another, vying for the restless clots of humanity flowing in and out and riding up and down the sandy stretch. From the saloons gushed a torrent of music, pianos, fiddles, guitars.

A shout tore the hum of the milling

throng. Martin drew rein.

Two men burst through a saloon's doors, mauling and gouging as they battled out into the street. Long-haired men, wild-eyed and savage. One reeled, only to spring forward with drawn knife. Two hard bodies thudded. A man screamed and slipped down, clutching his bloody throat, while the heaving knifer stood over him.

"He's bleedin' to death," an onlooker said simply.

Another man, as wild-looking as the antagonists, pawed a path through the crowd and stared at the man moaning and writhing on the ground. He drew his revolver and shot the knife-wielder, who fell backward and lay twitching.

"Go get the doc!" somebody shouted. But no one moved.

"Doc — hell," a man said a last. "Get a wagon — they're both goners."

Martin rode ahead. At Dodge he had seen men die, however none more violently than these. Even so, such a sight was always new and terrible and senseless.

More signs proclaimed Hillyard ownership of a busy wagon yard and livery stable, of a two-story hotel, the Hillyard House, and a mammoth general store. Lettering on the store's window read: OUTFITTING —

Loans — Hunting Guides — We Buy Hides. And below that, as if some discerning mind had decreed so for reasons of propriety and ethics, in smaller letters: *Attorney at Law.*

An impulse grew. Martin swung down, tied to the hitching rack and passed through the shifting crowd, slowing his step once inside, impressed by the abundance of merchandise, especially the racks of heavy rifles. Connecting rooms opened left and right off the main section of the store, all crowded with goods. Close by, smoked meat smell penetrated the pungent mingling of leather and cloth. Looking up, he saw long pieces of dark, rich meat suspended on a light rope. Buffalo tongues. A sudden hunger got into him. He'd buy one on his way out.

Martin was the only customer. A pale, harried clerk approached to wait on him, and Martin asked, "Is Mr. Hillyard in?"

A gleam of amusement came to the man's eyes and which he quickly crushed, leaving a suggestion of servility and fear. He said, "Go on back to the office," and, after a hasty glance rearward, began dusting a row of Wellington boots.

Martin, moving on, became aware of an atmosphere of unremitting industry and driving diligence. Past the gun racks two bookkeepers on high stools penned entries in thick, red-backed ledgers. Neither as much as glanced up when Martin walked by.

And immediately, sentry-like, a prim and angular woman rose from her tidy desk and eyed him severely, her movements more challenging than one of greeting or courteous inquiry.

"Yes?" she asked precisely, squeezing her exact lips together. She looked formidable behind her glasses. Her head was erect, in the high-collared vise of a white blouse.

"I'm here to see R. H. Hillyard," Martin said, hat in hand.

"May I ask your name and the nature of your business, sir?" Her voice sounded clipped, pure Bostonian.

He was beginning to feel the stir of annoyance. "Roebuck — Martin Roebuck — and I prefer to take up my business in person with Mr. Hillyard."

She measured him up and down, her gaze pecking away, assessing many things, and into her stiff expression crept the bare trace of a smile, much like the clerk's and also quickly erased. Meanwhile, the bookkeepers, who had turned their heads, seemed to enjoy the mild confrontation.

Turning briskly to an office door, she opened it and entered and closed it behind her. Before many moments she came out.

"You may go in, Mr. Roebuck," she said.

He opened the door and saw no one, his eyes on the book-lined wall before him. There was the faint scent of lilacs. Before he could turn, a rich voice spoke from his right:

"Please come in, Mr. Roebuck. I'm Ruby Hillyard."

Chapter 2

The woman he saw standing behind the desk of polished cherry wood could have been thirty, more or less. Her lustrous black hair was combed over her ears and coiled on the back of her head. Her olive skin set off large black eyes and a wide, full-lipped mouth. A woman neither large nor small, but well-proportioned. Not pretty, not beautiful. But an arresting, handsome woman, he thought. Her voice, however, did not seem to fit her. It sounded a trifle too emphatic, too matter of fact, an impression which faded as she met his gaze.

She stood before a large wall map of the state of Texas, into which, like feathered arrows, were stuck long pins trailing tiny streamers of red ribbon. She dropped a pin on the desk and said, somewhat wearily:

35

"I know . . . you were expecting a man instead of a woman, Mr. Roebuck. Won't you sit down?"

"I thought your secretary was going to demand my pedigree before she let me in," he said, waiting for her to be seated.

She noticed his manners. She said, "Miss Pettibone was trained in Boston's best school of business. She's also my accountant."

"She looks efficient."

"A woman storekeeper has to be out here, if she makes a go of it, Mr. Roebuck. Men like to do business with men. Over a bottle; in a saloon. That's why I use my initials. A good deal of my outfitting trade would escape me if I used my given name." She was frankly appraising him. "If it's a grubstake you want, I suppose you have letters of credit?"

"For once I don't need a loan," he replied and smiled reminiscently.

"All the better. That means you want wagons, supplies, mules, rifles, lead, powder, and you've been around town and compared prices and you want to know how R. H. Hillyard will deal with you." She had a businesslike manner of speaking, of suggesting and persuading, though all the while not letting a man forget her attractiveness. "There are still fortunes to be made on the buffalo range."

"I'm not after hides," he told her. Yet he was interested in hide-hunting, in a way, and he wondered why he evaded acknowledging his connections. "But I need a guide. A good one."

Her dark, even eyebrows arched up. "A guide, though you won't hunt?"

"An absolutely reliable man who knows the buffalo country."

She hesitated. "He may be difficult to find, Mr. Roebuck."

"In a town swarming with hunters?" he said, surprised. "The street out there is full of men."

"Yes — mostly renegades, outlaws. Army deserters, pariahs."

"I'm not concerned with a man's past, so long as he knows the country."

"You might be sorry. It's obvious you're new to the frontier. Why, you even have manners." She showed him a slight smile. "No — you don't want to hire one of those men out there." Her concern was convincing and intimate. It was equally frustrating.

He rose. "Can you or not furnish me a reliable guide?"

"The men who work through me are out on the range. So I'm afraid not, right now. No one I could trust. If I recommended a man and he didn't pan out, then you would blame me." Ruby Hillyard stood, a motion of dismissal which he found ruffling.

"I'll look around town," he said, walking to the door. There he faced her once more. "Maybe you know my partner?" he asked, on impulse, and a light sarcasm escaped him. "Guess I should say my former partner. He may trade with you. Trumbo? Sid Trumbo?"

She stood a little straighter and clasped her hands together. Her expression portrayed a mere curiosity. "Trumbo? Trumbo?" she repeated. "I've heard of him. I don't know him. And he may trade here with us. I don't know." Her voice communicated a casual interest, no more. "Hundreds of hunters operate out of Griffin, you know."

He thought she had finished. Instead, she said, "Buffalo country can be dangerous."

"Not half so dangerous as your town here. I saw two men killed just before I came in. Open country will look good to me again."

"Mr. Roebuck," she said, "you don't understand what I've been trying to tell you. I know. I'm the biggest outfitter in Texas. See those pins in the map? They show the location of hide crews in which I have an interest. So I know the situation out there. Believe me, it can be dangerous. There are Indians."

"Just Indians?" Her positiveness nettled

him. "The Eastern newspapers say hide-stealing and murder are on the increase since prices went up last fall."

"Exaggerations, Mr. Roebuck. Exaggerations. Blood-and-thunder creations of irresponsible correspondents. I suggest that instead of hiring a guide you know nothing about that you wait a few days. Or join some outfit. Or wait till I can find you a good man."

"I didn't come all the way from St. Louis just to wait."

"You may have to. You camped or staying in town?"

"Camped downriver."

"I'll get in touch with you."

"Never mind." He didn't believe her. He turned his back and left the office, his annoyance aggravated by her patronizing look as he went out.

He used the next hour looking over the town, had a drink in Mollie McCabe's Palace of Beautiful Sin, and another in the Planters' House. In Christianson's Gun Shop he saw a hunter sell his Big Fifty Sharps for twenty dollars, the surest indicator of all that the hide harvest was waning, and head for Huber's Saloon. At Conrad & Rath's Store, like Ruby Hillyard's, a sprawling catacomb of rooms stifled with merchandise, he heard complaints of slow business. "A year ago," one clerk said, "there'd be forty wagons lined up to be loaded, a hundred hunters in here buying supplies as fast as we could sell 'em."

Saloons were drawing the greatest share of trade, and what Martin had taken for traffic in and out of the stores was more the milling of hunters, bullwhackers, soldiers, and cowboys wandering from one whisky mill and bagnio to another.

From the doorway of the Bison Hotel an ample-bosomed woman played her sharp watchfulness over him. She rested one careless hand on her hip while she twirled the varicolored beads of a long necklace. Her red lips were heavy and slack. She fixed him a partial smile and he heard her low but distinct voice as an inviting murmur:

"Howdy, Lonesome. Come on in . . . the water's fine."

He glanced back at her and was walking on when a long-haired man, reeling and stumbling, eyes glazed, swayed up to her. "Say, girlie," he mumbled, "le's go a whirl." He barged toward the doorway, grabbing for her waist.

Swiftly, with a practiced alertness, she wheeled and caught his arm and swung him spinning across the boardwalk to sprawl in the street. The crowd hooted. Hands on hips, she snarled:

"Don't rough me — you lop-eared ba-boon! And you stink! You hunters *always* stink!"

The man got up, puzzled rather than angry. "Now, Lottie," he pleaded. "I just come into town for a little fun."

"Fun, hell! Take a bath first. Go to the creek. You know I run a respectable place."

In front of Huber's Saloon, two figures captured Martin's interest. Both humped on the walk's edge, an Indian in yellow shirt and derby hat, out of which slanted a red feather. A white man clothed in buckskins, slouch hat and moccasins. His hair, which dropped down his back, was silvery and wavy, and his white mustache hung in the mournful arc of an oxbow. Martin was re-minded of a character out of the Wild West acts one saw on the Eastern stages.

The white man would speak, using hand signs as well, and solemnly the Indian would nod, down and up, a mirthless grin on the broad slab of his face; and then he would speak and lift his hands to describe fluent air pictures. Both seemed unaware of their sur-roundings, lost in a remote world of their own.

As Martin walked closer, his humorous first impression changed. The Indian was in a state of drunken stupefaction. His attire

41

left him absurd and degraded. The white man was also on the brink of insensibility. His silvery hair was dirty, his elbows protruded through his greasy buckskin shirt and his mouth, mostly lost under the folds of his mustache and in the matting of gray whiskers covering chin and jaws, seeped brown tobacco stains down the corners.

Just then the Indian muttered, and the white man, stirring himself, replied in the same guttural tongue.

Martin was passing Conrad & Rath's again when the thought caught up with him. He drew around. The white man back there was speaking the Indian's language and using Indian signs.

Martin took only a minute or two returning to the corner and along Main Street to Huber's Saloon. His expectancy dropped away. The Indian occupied the same position on the walk, but the long-haired man in dirty buckskins wasn't there. Nor was he on the street, nor in Huber's. Coming outside, Martin looked up at the sky. The afternoon was about gone.

He rode the river road, thinking that the town had declined mainly to whoop and holler. Although prices held high, far fewer hides were being hauled to market than last fall. Hunters reported riding farther and farther for game. Men now hanging around Griffin would have been on the buffalo range a few months ago, shooting and skinning. Cattle-raising was the coming venture as the country gradually emptied. Longhorns were filling the gap left by the buffalo. So he had gathered from his rounds in the saloons and stores, listening to the grumbles.

He could smile at Ruby Hillyard's remarks about easy money killing buffalo, when she knew the hide game was past its peak and then some. Spotting him for a greenhorn, she had voiced high prospects in hopes of selling him a costly outlay. Still, he decided, poor hunting didn't explain everything. Why, in bitter anger and hurt, he must travel so far for an accounting of what was rightfully his, earned when the tide of slaughter ran high.

The high ridges to the west masked all but the sun's afterglow when Martin took the old Indian woman's supper to her. She was sitting cross-legged in the entrance of the little tent, face turned to the rising wind. And he thought: all wild things range into the wind. She was becoming stronger; he saw that and something more, a difference, as he handed her the tin plate: an estimate between mere tolerance and controlled hostility for him in her expression.

When purple darkness flooded the plain below the ridges, Augustin went to his tent and Martin climbed inside the wagon, pulled off boots, shirt, and trousers, and stretched out on the pallet bed in his underwear. The stillness held around the camp, and then, gradually, the muttering undertone of the town reached him across the warm night. He heard a shot; another.

Griffin, he mused, had just the kind of honey to draw Sid Trumbo. A town without order or scruples, ruthless and wild and cruel. Drawing women like Lottie, who could throw a man with the skill of a wrestler, and good-looking Ruby Hillyard, who was just as formidable in other ways. And the silvery-haired man in greasy buckskins. Martin thought of him last, before he turned on his side and fell into a dreamless sleep.

He roused up to utter darkness, thrown roughly awake, hearing Tack's growl of warning under the wagon. No other close by sounds. Even the raucous hum of the town was muffled. His groping fingers touched the case of the Sharps .40-90, then found the six-shooter. He froze as Tack growled again.

Horses were padding softly down the sandy river road.

Martin relaxed, thinking the riders would pass. But the shuffling hoofs ceased, re-

sumed in moments, ceased and picked up
again, traveling slower each time, bringing
cautious ripples of sound.

Tack was growling without letup. Martin
pulled on his trousers, crawled to the tailgate and dropped to the ground, feeling the
sandy soil under his bare feet. Tack, his
whine just audible, drew beside him. Martin
laid his left hand on the broad head for silence. The big dog quit whining. A low
growl settled in his throat.

Martin could see nothing against the black
line of river-bank timber and he heard
nothing, so he knew the horsemen had
halted again. Therefore, he wasn't expecting
the furious slash of hoofs directly beyond the
camp, nor the ear-stunning gunshots and the
blue flames winking in the darkness.

Crouched down, he heard bullets slam
the wagon's side-boards. He fired back at
the dim mass. A man yelled in pain. By then
the riders were pounding down the road.

Late, Martin remembered the old woman.
He started up, hearing behind him the un-
broken eloquence of Augustin cursing in
French.

Hurrying to the tent, Martin made out a
figure in the opening. "You all right?" he
called. She answered instantly, a high-
pitched gabble of excitement. Although he

45

didn't understand, her tone said she was unharmed, and it came to him that for the first time he thought of her as a real person.

Augustin ran up and bent down, striking a match. "Look! She fight with the stick. *Beaucoup*."

Indeed, Martin saw. She was crouched in the doorway, savagely determined, a stick in each hand. A laughable sight under less serious circumstances.

"The sticks?" Augustin asked. "Why she get them?"

"She didn't trust us, maybe."

He was up early and riding again for the settlement. It reminded him of a shaggy old renegade, sluggish after a night's carousing and just now stirring.

The yawning barkeep in Huber's listened without expression while Martin described the white-haired man in buckskins.

"Oh, him?" the man said finally and his voice sounded indifferent. "You mean old Rip Burke. Calls himself Buffalo Burke."

"Is he really a hunter?"

"Was, till the bottle got him. Nobody'll hire him any more."

"Where can I find him?"

"Well, it won't be at the Hillyard House or the Planters'. Look out behind the saloon."

Martin could hardly conceive that in the

allcy's litter of crates, boxes, paper, whisky barrels, bottles, and garbage he would find so many inert figures — two white men and the yellow-shirted Indian of yesterday, the treasured derby securely on his head. Martin looked at the other lax faces without recognition.

Somewhere a man was singing in a blurred and happy voice, up and down, obviously pleased with the tuneless sounds he was making; for he would reach a squeaky pitch and dwell there, enjoying the discord, and afterward, as pleased, slide downward to bull-frog depths.

A frowzy-haired woman jutted her head out a window of the Palace of Beautiful Sin and shrilled, "Shut up — you goddamned old caterwaulin' tomcat!"

A moment of silence, but only a moment. Cantankerously the voice rose again, louder and more discordant. Still, Martin saw no one. He started along the alley, drawn toward a low shed behind the Palace, came around the shed and stopped.

There sat his man in greasy buckskins, hatless, back propped against the wall, ringed by a cordon of empty whisky bottles. He looked dirtier than the day before, if that was possible. He could be fifty, Martin guessed, or sixty-five. His trembling left

47

hand gripped a bottle showing shallow amber liquid; into it his trembling right hand struggled to drain another bottle. He was singing as he worked, an intense concentration warping his bearded face:

"Oh, 'twas in the town of Jacksboro, in the spring of seventy-three,
A man by th' name of Crego came a-steppin' up to me —"

One precious golden drop spilled and he cursed bitterly, fluently. His eyes strayed to Martin's boots and up. He blinked.

"Morning, Mr. Burke," Martin said.

The old man said, "Collectin' my morning toddy," and, closing one eye, squinted down the barrel of the left-hand bottle. "Ain't much. These barkeeps get stingier every day. They forget when a man had all the makin's."

"I'd like to talk to you, Mr. Burke."

"Me? 'Bout what?" Distrust laced the gruff voice.

"Let's have a drink in Huber's, then breakfast, and I'll tell you about it."

"A drink, you say?" At the word old Rip Burke was transformed and on his feet in a twinkling, his step agile. Bending a reproachful glare on the left-hand bottle, he drained it at one short gulp, and as he wiped his mouth with the back of his hand a remnant of pride seemed to rise up in him. He said, "I God — how'd you know my name? You're a plumb total stranger to me. What's your handle?"

"Martin Roebuck."

"Never heard tell of you. What's your notion?"

Martin delayed, asking himself how you reached so cross-grained a character. "I need your help," he said earnestly. "It won't be much trouble, and I'll pay you for your time."

Suspicion glittered in the bleary, light blue eyes. "Pay me for what?"

"You speak Indian, don't you?"

"First off," Burke replied, adopting a superior tone, "there's more'n one kind of Injun talk."

"I'm aware of that. Yesterday I saw you talking to an Indian."

"Tonkawa Jack? We're old friends. I gave him his hat." A scowl plowed the dissipated face. "What about it? What's wrong with me talkin' to an old friend?"

"Nothing," Martin said, keeping his voice amiable. Already much of his expectation had ebbed. "Only you said Tonkawa. Can you talk Comanche?"

Burke sneered. "You ain't been in town long, have you, young sprout? I God, yes, I can jabber Comanch'. If I didn't, I could talk to 'em in sign. I can spit a little Spanish, too. Now what's the lay?"

"After a drink and breakfast," Martin dickered.

Burke pulled on his chin whiskers and crossed his arms and screwed his face into a facsimile of pondering, of weighing the proposition. It was important, Martin sensed, to wait, to let the old man protect his little hoard of pride.

"Breakfast?" Burke considered, after another pause. "Reckon I could eat a little bite."

At the Planters' House Burke began putting away stacks of flapjacks, bowls of hominy grits, a platter of buffalo steak swimming in brown gravy and a mound of biscuits, in between cup after cup of black coffee, and speaking not once. Half an hour later, he pushed back from the table, swiped a greasy sleeve across his mouth, and said:

"Got a smoke on you?"

Martin handed him a cigar.

Burke sniffed it suspiciously, then nodded. "Got a match?"

Martin gave him a match which Burke, in a single, looping swipe, struck on the seat of his buckskins. He lighted up, inhaled and through a cloud of smoke demanded, "Now what's the lay?"

Martin started at the beginning, sparing few details, and when he had finished, Burke scoffed, "You just want me to talk to the old woman — that it?"

"I want you to find out something about her."

A cynical wryness curled the cave of Burke's mouth in the clump of dirty gray whiskers. "So you can git rid of her?"

"So I can locate her people, her band," Martin said distinctly and saw Burke's ill-concealed disbelief.

"How much is in it?" the old man asked, a slyness gathering in his eyes.

"Twenty dollars."

"Fifty."

"Fifty!" Martin exploded. "You're holding me up."

Burke's chair scraped as he stood. "It's fifty or nothin'. I God, I've seen the day when I wouldn't scratch my butt end for that little dab."

"Times have changed, Mr. Burke. Else you'd be out hunting."

"Maybe times have," Burke swore. "But I ain't. Take it or hump it, Roebuck." Erect, eyes flaring, he started off.

"Twenty-five," Martin offered, thinking that would slow the old man. It did not. "Thirty," Martin said, louder.

Burke faltered in step, but not too soon, and swung about, but not too eagerly, and appeared to cogitate at great length.

"Guess you're a square shooter after all, Roebuck," he said finally, in a tentative way that hinted he might be suspending judgment still. "Buffalo Burke never was one to come up on a man's hind side when he was in a tight. It's a deal, and the breakfast was fine. Drinks, too. I'll ride out with you."

He smiled, then, a bit crookedly, and thrust out his brown hand, and looking into the raffish features, Martin knew that old Rip Burke had taken him as neatly as the greenest rube.

A side-saddled horse stood tied near the wagon when Martin and Burke rode up. As they dismounted, Augustin canted his head toward the shelter tent. "She come to see *grand-mère*."

Martin looked. Harriet Sanford was just taking leave of the old woman. He and Burke walked out to her. "Don't go yet, Miss Sanford. Mr. Burke, here, speaks Comanche. He's going to interpret for me."

"Thank you. I'd like to listen."

The Comanche's dark eyes turned wary, and she held Harriet Sanford's gifts closer against her, a nice comb and looking glass, plainly fearful that these white men might seize them from her.

Martin winced at her naked distrust.

Burke spoke and her coppery, intricately wrinkled face, as though worn away by the years of sun and wind, and which Martin was accustomed to seeing in inscrutable impassiveness, flashed out of its mask. She replied at once and her eyes lighted up, her exclaiming voice all high-pitched pleasure.

Burke threw Martin a told-you-so look and sat, cross-legged, Indian style. Augustin brought a camp stool, for Miss Sanford.

"Tell her," Martin began, kneeling to listen, "I will ask the pony soldiers to take her back to her tribe on the reservation near Fort Sill."

Burke spoke to her and also used his hands, pointing north, adding many unnecessary flourishes, it seemed. He was, Martin saw, taking satisfaction in his role, as the central figure of this scene, like an actor made important by the line she alone knew.

Her answer followed rapidly, sonorous and flowing to Martin's ears, characterized by rolling *r*'s.

"She says no *bueno,*" Burke said. "She won't go to the soldiers' houses near Medicine Bluff. That's Fort Sill."

"Why not?"

"Claims the soldiers will kill her. To her notion all white men are mean." Burke chuckled. "Ain't she a corker? Mighty smart. Her name is Mary White Butterfly. A woman of one of the Broad Hats at Fort Sill named her that."

"Tell her I promise the pony soldiers won't harm her."

"Think she'd believe you?" Burke sneered.

"Tell her anyway," Martin snapped, beginning to lose patience.

Shrugging, Burke complied. Her reply fairly crackled. Burke grinned like a badger. "Guess you savvied that. She don't trust white men — no white man."

"Remind her," Martin told him, "that we can make her go."

Burke gave Martin a blank stare. "If her band ain't there?"

"Well, where are her people?"

The old woman released a barrage of Comanche and her hands cut fluent meanings, so intense that Martin understood somewhat: *Far away.* Withered hands close to her head, the index fingers curved for horns. *Buffalo.*

"She belongs to a little band of Kwahadi," Burke explained. "Staked Plains Comanch'. Soldiers'd call 'em renegades b'cause they left the reservation to hunt buff'lo. They're way west or northwest by now. Everybody was mighty hungry last she saw."

Martin stood and thrust both hands into his pockets, frustration balled up inside him. Likely, through Lieutenant Egan, she could be transported to Fort Sill whether she agreed or not, cruel as that might seem. He shook off the thought for the moment and turned to find her watching him, the black eyes fixed on him like barb points.

"Tell her," he said to Burke, "I'll buy her a good gentle horse. Blankets and food. So she can rejoin her people on the Plains." He noticed Miss Sanford again. She was leaning forward, her evident sympathy as a cloak thrown around the gesturing old woman.

For as Burke talked, a sudden animation swept the savage face. Her birdlike mouth quivered in answer. She gazed off, a distant look in her eyes. The leathery lips became pensive. She turned her head and considered Martin in a new and obscure way, without the customary contempt, and he had his first hope that she would agree.

"She says she's too old to ride that many sleeps," Burke muttered. "First place, she can't go back. Her band left her to die. Threw her away —"

"— but," Martin interrupted, "wouldn't they take care of her?"

"You don't know the Comanch', Roebuck. How superstitious they be. She's a ghost to them — already dead. Why, if she rode into their camp, you'd see the quickest cloud of dust ever; them a-makin' it." He folded his arms and shook his head. "She's dead. She can't go back."

Martin could see that Burke was more hindrance than help. If only for cantankerous reasons, he favored the old woman.

"You know a good deal about Indians," Martin said, thinking to shine Burke's vanity. "That's easy to see. So I'll ask you. What can I do with her?"

"Never heard tell of this fix 'fore now. Beats me."

"All right," Martin said. "Then ask *her*."

The unforeseen question left Burke without a reply, but he and the old woman were soon swapping words and signs, and then he said:

"She says dump her by the Tonkawa camp. Her hair is poor. But the Tonks can have it."

"You know I can't do that."

"If you won't, she says take her out on the prairie. Leave her there. Throw her away, same as her people did, b'cause she's old. She don't care. It's Comanch' custom."

Martin flung up a hand. "Nonsense."

56

"What you aim to do with her? She's got a right to know."

"Tell her" — Martin began haltingly — "tell her I won't throw her away." Tomorrow, he thought, would be soon enough to take her to the fort.

He looked away, stung by disappointment. It was intolerable that one old woman, a cast-off of her own people, should delay him. Burke and Miss Sanford rose. All three went slowly to the wagon. There, of a sudden, Martin turned on Burke:

"How far to Double Mountain?"

"Week's ride or so."

"Can you guide me there?"

Burke cocked one bleary eye like a spy-glass. "Depends."

"On what — money?"

"More on where 'bouts around Double Mountain you aim to go."

"Sid Trumbo's camp." Burke's gaze deepened, and Martin said, "You know him?"

"Who don't?"

"Afraid of him?"

Burke swung in, his stubbly jaw jutting. "Me — Buffalo Burke — scared o' the likes o' him?" He tried to swagger, and in doing so he swayed, off balance, and had to catch himself.

"In that case," Martin said, "there's no reason why you can't guide me, is there?"

"You a friend of Trumbo's?"

"I didn't say."

Burke's bluster faded, leaving him uncertain and evasive. "You won't like that country," he predicted, falling back on an old man's positiveness. "Ain't the game there used to be. Water's a problem more times than not. Be Comanch' or Kioways, sure. Thunderstorms and sandstorms. Wolves, bedbugs, flies. Millions o' flies. Man can hardly eat himself a meal." And as though having exhausted his principal objections, he must find another: "Buffalo Burke ain't guidin' no outfit with a woman along. That's gospel. I didn't say so at the time, but she claims she's got powers."

"More of her nonsense," Martin said. "And she's not going. I intend to leave her at the fort."

"Mr. Roebuck." The clear and pleasant voice calling his name reminded him that he had all but forgotten Harriet Sanford. "I think I have a better way," she said, revealing a sudden, brilliant smile. "She can stay with me while you're gone."

"You mean that?"

Feeling pinked her cheeks. "I wouldn't offer if I didn't mean it. I've rented a house on Fourth Street."

"She won't sleep in a white man's house."

"You can put up her tent in the back yard."

She was very much in earnest. He could see that resolution in her eyes and in the firmness of her mouth.

"I don't believe you realize what you'd be taking on," he said.

"It would be inhuman to leave her at the fort, even if the soldiers let you."

"Why?"

"There, surrounded by her enemies? She'd be frightened every moment."

He rubbed a forefinger up and down on his cheekbone, considering the truth in her observation. "When, then?"

"This afternoon. Tomorrow."

"Tomorrow morning on our way out," Martin said.

Chapter 3

He stood by the wagon, watching her ride off, and feeling some degree of guilt, as if he had imposed upon her compassion; for she was young, possessing sympathy and under-standing for all people, still believing in their potential goodness.

A buggy was dashing down the middle of the narrow road. The driver did not pull over. Harriet Sanford had to swerve her mount aside. The buggy, its wheels spinning yellow sand, its leather top glistening in the sunlight, rushed on behind a high-stepping sorrel. A woman drove: Ruby Hillyard.

She reined in the nervous animal not far from the wagon, her eyes taking in the Comanche woman before her tent, and the shaggy, growling dog. When she saw Martin, she drove off the road and Martin, unhurriedly, walked out.

"Quite a collection you have here," she said, playing a curious look on the Indian woman.

He offered no explanation, remembering how she had held to the center of the road and forced Harriet off.

"I came to tell you I'm trying to find a guide for you," she said, after a moment.

"I've hired a man," he said, thinking that would end the discussion.

"Who?"

"Rip Burke. Over there."

Burke was squatted down, in an animated conversation with Augustin. She looked and said, "You'll regret it. He's as unreliable as a Tonkawa. A drunk. A braggart."

"I'll keep him sober enough."

Her instantaneous laughter dispelled the businesslike quality of her voice and caused

60

Martin to become more aware of her attractiveness.

"I really came to repair any false impressions you might have had of me yesterday," she said, lowering her eyes. "Maybe you'll let me show you the sights, such as they are?"

"You always do this for strangers?"

She laughed again, a close, inviting sound. "Of course. What really bothers me is I think I was unfair, even rude to you. They say that's one of my many failings and I admit it." He found her frankness becoming to her. She sounded like a woman now instead of a Yankee merchant. She said, "So if you'd like, I'll show you around," and she made room for him on the padded seat.

He wasn't so naïve that he believed her explanation for coming here. At the same time he could feel her unmistakable vitality. He got in.

She sent the long-legged gelding swiftly down the road. "This trotter cost me more than I'll ever tell," she said. "He's straight out of Maine. I love to go fast."

"Always taking the middle of the road?"

She replied immediately. "You're thinking of that girl back there. I almost didn't see her in time, I was so intent on finding your camp."

Beneath the spinning buggy wheels the road, winding with the river, lost its identity and dwindled to wagon tracks. The last camp fell behind. The trail bent sharply and straightened, and ahead, on a broad flat, Martin saw an enormous white mound.

"My bone pile," Ruby Hillyard said, as though amused at herself. "Makes good fertilizer for your worn-out Eastern farms. People used to laugh at me. They don't any more, with bones bringing six to eight dollars a ton in Fort Worth and Denison." Her satisfaction quickened. "I'm buying more government-type heavy wagons, big enough to haul up to five tons. My men have learned to beat that by placing pelvic bones along the edge of the loaded wagon box and piling higher." She reined up, still contemplating the gray mass. A defensiveness . . . down-pitched her voice. "Nothing is wasted. Hoofs for glue. Horns make nice buttons, knife handles, and combs. Won't even be that one of these days."

"And just yesterday," he said, in light sarcasm, "you painted the high prospects of hide-hunting, the waiting fortunes."

"Prospects," she said, unabashed, "are *always* good when you think ahead. There are still plenty of buffalo to kill — if you go far enough and know where to go. Still plenty of money to be made."

"You're still selling. And with fewer hides

brought to market, prices are better than ever, aren't they? When I left St. Louis, choice winter robes were quoted at seven-fifty, laid down in Fort Worth."

Her face underwent a knowing change. "You know something about hides, don't you?"

"I used to hunt, and I still do some buying."

Scented and cool, the breath of a soft breeze strayed along the stream. The stridence of the upriver camps, dulled by distance, lay muted and lazy to the ear. And Ruby Hillyard's half-smile could mean many things. She was a damned fine-looking woman and also a determined one.

"You led me to think you were a greenhorn," she said.

"Maybe you assumed it because I didn't smell like a hunter. Well, I used to."

She took up the reins in her gloved hands, the sorrel moved out, circling, and they trotted briskly along the river. When Martin's camp appeared, he expected her to turn in. She did not and he said nothing. Coming to the crossing, she turned eastward and, on the other side, took a trail-like road leading southeast.

He smelled wood smoke and soon saw tipis and brush huts dotting a clearing. There were naked children, squaws carrying wood and water, and unmoving bucks, and swarms of flies and numberless gaunt dogs.

Ruby Hillyard hurried the sorrel through the odorous camp and was turning around when Martin said, "Why come here?"

"Visitors *always* come to look at the Tonkawa camp. Did you ever see more miserable creatures?"

"You can't say their manners aren't good. They didn't gawk at us the way white people would."

Her pique flashed and went out. Her strong face grew reflective. She snapped the buggy whip. She dashed through the camp to the main road, rushed along it to the crossing and tarried on the west side of the Clear Fork in the speckled shade.

She looked across at him, bringing the scent of lilacs. "What you said back there marks you as a man who doesn't understand Indians or the frontier. I wonder if you aren't a pilgrim after all?"

"The Tonks remind me of the Kaws in Kansas, and the answer comes out the same in either case: Indians don't fare well away from the buffalo, trying to live like white people."

She swung left, giving the sorrel its proud head all the way to Martin's camp. The old

Indian woman hadn't changed position in front of her tent. Ruby Hillyard's curious voice rose, "Where in the world did you get her?"

"Coming in off the main trail." He said no more and got down and thanked her, adding, "I like your fine gelding. If you paid less than two thousand, you stole him at night."

She responded to the obvious flattery. "So I stole him — for twelve hundred — and it was in daylight." Still, she did not go. He could see the dark eyes exploring his face and he could feel himself reacting to her full appraisal.

"Guess I'm just too bold for a woman," she said. "Another one of my failings. Will you come to dinner this evening?"

A moment. "Why?"

"Do I have to give a reason?"

He lifted one shoulder and smiled back at her, not understanding why he hesitated unless it was instinct.

"Will you, Mr. Roebuck?" She tilted her head a certain way as she said it.

"Name's Martin. It will be a pleasure, Miss Hillyard."

"Ruby. Call me Ruby . . . Seven o'clock at the Hillyard House. Go to the desk."

Rip Burke was waiting for his pay, slouched against a wagon wheel. Martin paid him and said, "Made up your mind about guiding me to Trumbo's camp?"

"Be one hell of a trip," Burke said, discouraging. "Wolves, bedbugs, flies —"

"Millions of 'em," Martin mimicked.

"True."

"Well?"

"Have to have ten dollars a day with grub."

"Too high, but I'll pay it."

"You sound in a hurry."

"I am."

"It's a deal," Burke said, offering his hand. Martin took it. Burke looked at the money in his left hand and an anticipatory thirst glided over his face.

"We leave in the morning," Martin warned. "Load up supplies this afternoon. You be here around daybreak. If you get drunk, I'll hunt you down and tie you to your saddle."

Burke rocked back on his heels and his lips rolled together. But behind the rheumy eyes lurked a glimmer of respect, Martin thought, or was it amusement?

"I'll be here," Burke said.

The long-haired clerk at the Hillyard House looked out of his environment, recently arrived from the buffalo range, rough and square of face, wind-burned to the color of a saddle seat; and after a bath, always a questionable assumption, a wrestling bout muscling into the coat cramping his burly shoulders and arms.

He spoke in a toneless voice, "Miss Ruby will see you now," and directed Martin to the second floor. At Martin's rap a Mexican woman opened the door, took his hat and disappeared, her footsteps soundless on the mossy carpeting.

Martin didn't move. After the lusty clatters and smells of boisterous Griffin Avenue, these surroundings seemed imagined. The profusion of unexpected richness, the opulence, elegant for the frontier, though a high-born sophisticate would no doubt consider as unrefined the stuffed, red velvet sofa and its curving, hand-carved back, and the bright red carpeting and its patterns of yellow roses, and the red velvet drapes, and the china lamps likewise decorated with yellow roses. And probably a patron of the arts in St. Louis would sniff at the oil painting, which showed a group of nude Arcadian maidens, coyly seen at a distance, as they watched their flocks by a blue waterfall.

Over the room the coal-oil lamps shed an amber intimacy which turned Martin's thoughts away from the raucous echoes of the town. He sat on the sofa, only to rise at the rustling of a dress.

"Good evening, Martin."

"Evening, Miss Hillyard."

"My name's Ruby, remember? And the H stands for Hope."

Fluttering a feathered fan, she held out her left hand in greeting and Martin, bowing over it, drew in the subtle lilac fragrance of her. She was even more striking tonight, her parted black hair drawn down over her ears and gathered low on her neck, and the dark eyes and the full mouth, and her bare shoulders in the deep green dress, trimmed in white lace.

The Mexican woman brought a tray of glasses and bottles and a silver bowl. "What would you like?" Ruby Hillyard asked.

"Rye if you have it."

"I do. Though most men out here drink bourbon whisky."

Martin nodded and out of the past, floating by for no particular reason, he recalled to himself that Sid Trumbo had been a rye drinker when he could get it.

"I even have ice," she said.

"Ice?"

"I have my own ice house."

Presently late evening's purple replaced the pale dimness outside the windows, and the town's throaty turbulence lost distinctness, dwindling to a murmurous unrest. The robust rye whisky began to warm Martin. A sense of comfort stole over him.

And again he was aware of her as a woman, full-bodied and forceful and sure of herself. At the same time he knew also there had to be non-apparent reasons for inviting him here. He watched her sipping red wine, her attention obliquely upon him.

She said, "You're still wondering why I invited you."

"I am a little curious," he said, smiling.

"Let's say I decided you are a gentleman, a rare breed in these parts."

He raised one hand in a warding-off gesture. "Spare me that. The so-called gentlemen I've run across were more fops than men." He took a swallow from the glass. "I'll remember your hospitality when I'm in buffalo country."

"You're leaving in the morning?"

"In a few days," he said, skirting a direct answer which, he realized, he had not concealed.

Ruby Hillyard set down her empty glass with a tiny tink. "You don't trust me, do you?"

"As much as you trust me."

Her pelting laughter drifted across the room and he laughed in turn. Color flushed her throat and cheeks, accenting her vivid qualities.

"I like a man who says what he thinks,"

she said. Rising, she went to the dark window, a compelling, rustling movement which drew Martin to stand behind her. Outside, the yellow eyes of the town glared up at them and the brawling hoarseness sounded nearer.

Gazing out there, she seemed to be thinking of distant events. "When the hides stop coming in, this town will die," she said. "It will die almost overnight, the way it was born." She moved, a gradual turning of her body toward him. Her flawless skin looked olive in the half-light. "But that is not tonight," she said and lifted her face to him.

He took her arms and kissed her, a tentative kiss. Her lips were a pleasure, also perfunctory and yet not too careless, an appraisal behind them.

It was she who drew back. "Why leave so soon?"

"Why wait?"

Just then the Mexican woman entered the room and glanced questioningly at her mistress. Annoyance shot through Ruby Hillyard's features. Her lips looked heavy and red. Her eyes changed, darkening. The Mexican woman left at once. Ruby sat on the sofa and Martin took a chair.

"Waiting," she said, her long fingers spreading the green skirt, "is something a woman learns. Men are unpredictable. They come and go with the wind." Her bold eyes were inquiring. "You're not married?"

He shook his head.

She studied him with a keener perception. "What happened? Another man beat your time?"

"She died before we were married."

"Oh . . ." She sank back, closed her eyes and opened them slowly. "I'm sorry. I don't think I meant that."

"You didn't. Besides, you didn't know."

The heaviness rose to her lips. "My husband deserted me when I was sixteen. Four weeks before our baby died." Martin stared at her sharply, in sudden sympathy. Her mouth twisted in self-contempt. "I didn't say that to get you on my side; it slipped out." She picked up his empty glass and hers, filled them and came back, murmuring. "If a woman waits too long, life will pass her by. She's got to act on her own. I educated myself. Learned to keep books. Studied law. I've made investments in the East. No man did that for me. I ask nothing of anyone."

"Aren't you a little harsh on the world?"

"Not harsh enough. Men are floaters and drifters, always looking for an easy thing." She emptied the wineglass. Into her eyes Martin saw a jeering and scoffing form against him. "It's hard to believe you were ever a buffalo hunter," she said. "Why didn't you stick with it? Too rough?"

"I don't believe I said."

His lack of anger puzzled her. "Believe me, the men in this town will break you if you stay here long enough."

"Ah," he said, turning his own irony on her, "the brave men you have here. Such as those who shot up my camp last night and rushed away."

"Guess somebody got tanked up." She looked surprised.

He let go a short laugh. "They'd ride that far downriver for fun? No. Not with plenty of other camps closer to shoot at."

A gap of silence widened between them. She offered no answer. Without speaking, she filled the glasses again, and when she returned he saw that her taunting of him was over, and the butting of her will against his, and her drawing him out.

"God," she breathed, and in that moment she looked like any woman. "It can get lonely in a hell hole like this. The sweat, the stink, the brawls."

"Even when you're making money?"

"Even when you're making money," she repeated. A slackness took over her face. It brought out hidden lines, suggesting in the years ahead a heavy, loose-fleshed woman, though she would always attract men. Attention to her dress and person hid those signs now.

She called for the Mexican woman to serve dinner and they ate under candle light and drank chilled wine, their conversation general and desultory.

It was late when Martin rose to leave and thanked Ruby Hillyard, whose animation of the early evening had returned.

"You're a fool for going out there," she said, "if you don't intend to hunt. There's nothing else."

He evaded a reply and turned to the door. She placed her hand on the knob ahead of him, paused and swung deliberately about and looked up at him, half-smiling, offering her lips to him again.

She drew against him, not heavily, and he bent his head. His arms went around her, feeling the firmness of her body. A sensation not felt the first time he kissed her flowed through her lips to his. He thought he sensed something there for him, if he desired it, something deeper and beyond her pretense; but he wasn't sure. This time it was he who stood back.

"Will you come to see me again?" she asked.

"You mean things will be the same later as they are now?"

Her half-smiling expression didn't waver. He thought he saw the invitation there once more, and then he went out.

Crossing the lobby, he saw a different clerk behind the desk. Men were still on the prowl at this late hour, going and coming, tramping the boardwalk. Several drummers occupied the wide chairs by the windows.

Martin stepped outside and stood on the crowded walk, catching the wash of voices along the street, and the wild-cat music soaring out of the saloons, and the sliding scrape of boots on rough dance floors. A woman was laughing, a shrill and continuous mirth, on the verge of hysteria.

A man on the walk opposite Martin gave a short, keen whistle.

Two drunks staggered into the hotel's buff-colored light. Arms locked for mutual support, singing a tuneless song, they weaved from side to side as they tried to navigate the walk. They strayed toward Martin. He stepped out of their way. They continued to weave in his direction. He stepped clear again, almost to the wall of the hotel.

One man bumped him and mumbled. Martin pushed him off. The man swayed back, using the point of his shoulder. Martin tensed, sensing the change even as he saw it, the mock amiability and discordant singing gone. Now he saw the pair separate and advance on him.

Martin took a blow alongside his head that slammed him against the wooden wall. He reacted on instinct, shielding his face until his head cleared, taking other smashes on his forearms and middle.

He swung at a bobbing face and felt his fist strike throat muscles. The man gagged and fell away. His partner tore in, thick and squat, boots pounding, arms swinging. Martin wheeled, punching for the blur of the face and missing. For a bit there was distance between them, and in that time Martin heard men running out of the hotel and the saloon next door.

The man lowered his head and bulled in. Martin felt pain as his wind was knocked out of him, felt himself being rammed toward the wall. He brought his arms up, broke the hold and drove the man back and stopped flat-footed to pull for breath, aware of faces ringing him. He stood in the center facing the two. They were hunters, he knew by their rancid stink.

One rushed him and Martin hit him. It was a solid blow to the head that jumped pain up Martin's arm. The man spun down.

Martin swung to meet the second man. They thudded together and bounced apart.

Hearing a shout from the crowd, Martin saw the first man on one knee in front of the doorway. He was wobbling up with a knife.

A figure lunged from the circle and kicked the knife loose. "You damned fool — no —"

"Kyle — what the hell?"

"Go on!"

The hunter got up and lost himself in the crowd. When Martin looked for the other man, he was gone, too.

Martin was wiping blood off his mouth and hacking for wind, when the one called Kyle strode past him into the Hillyard House. It was the burly, square-faced clerk who earlier had directed him to Ruby Hillyard's rooms.

Martin was surprised when Rip Burke showed up after daybreak, reeking of busthead shortly whisky, and what he called his "war bag" tied behind the cantle of his saddle and a battered Ballard carbine, its stock wrapped in rawhide, slung in a short boot. And he rode a different horse, causing Martin to wonder. A snuffy bay showed the markings of mustang blood, light of build, short hack, sound legs, fox ears and intelligent eyes.

"Didn't think I'd make it, did you, Roebuck?" Burke challenged, hands shaking, as he ferried a cup of Augustin's steaming coffee to his mouth.

"I knew you'd better."

The house on Fourth Street was an adobe, enclosed within a picket fence. Behind the house stood a shed and pole corral. Harriet Sanford came out on the porch as the rumbling wagon drew up, a gentle brown mare tied behind.

Martin dismounted and motioned for the old woman to come down. She only looked at him. He gestured again, seeing her perplexed unwillingness. She gave in all at once and descended on her own and, when Martin pointed to the gate she obeyed with slow steps, her moccasins husking over the packed earth. She did not understand until she noticed Harriet; that discovery wiped away her fear and bewilderment, manifest from the moment Martin had taken down the tent, folded it and made the sign for Go.

Opening the gate, Harriet took the old woman's arm for assurance and said, "Welcome. Welcome," and the old one returned a grimacing smile of pleasure, understanding, moving her head up and down.

Then, sighting the white man's strange house, she held back, dread and suspicion standing in her eyes. Martin told Augustin to bring the little tent, and when she saw it, a familiar thing, her face changed back and she entered the yard. All the men began unloading groceries. Martin made certain the new blankets were included.

"What's all this?" Harriet asked, wide-eyed.

"I'm not dumping her on you," Martin explained. "The mare is hers, too. When she gets stronger, maybe she'll ride back to her people. I can't swallow this idea they won't look after her."

"I can. I think she told Mr. Burke the truth. They threw her away. She has no home."

"In that case it's up to the Army, and taking her to the reservation."

"She's too weak to travel anywhere just now," Harriet Sanford said and turned to the old woman. The tent came first. When it was pitched in the back yard and the Comanche woman sat in the doorway, not unlike a small bronze statue, and the brown mare stood in the corral, Harriet invited the men into the house. New curtains hung at the windows. Martin breathed the ravening smell of baking bread.

She took them into a room arranged as the parlor, and afterward brought them coffee. "What do you call the Indian lady?" she asked. "Mary White Butterfly?"

"Augustin calls her *grand-mere*," Martin said, smiling over the term. "I think we ought to have an understanding. Soon as we get back, in about two weeks or so, I promise to take her off your hands. I mean I'll see that the Army does. That agreeable?"

"A way will be found, Mr. Roebuck," came the unperturbed reply. "I'm to meet my father in Rath City when he tells me to come out. Knowing him" — her voice had a forebearing patience — "that may be some time. I'm tempted to go to Rath and wait." She broke off her musing and Martin saw the hazel gaze inquiringly upon him. "Even ask you to take me with you, since Rath is south of Double Mountain."

"Buffalo country is no place for a woman."

I've camped out a great deal with my father. Up the Missouri River. In the Rockies."

The hazel stare pierced him. He said, giving ground, "And the Indian woman?"

"A way would be found, just as you've found a way so far."

"I won't take you," he replied in the next moment, getting up, and saw a flicker of disappointment pass across her face.

As Augustin headed the team toward the road leading around the fortress bluff, Martin, following beside Burke, looked back and saw Harriet Sanford standing on the porch.

She waved. He waved back and in imagination he could see again the lineaments of her face as she asked him to take her with him. By the corner of the house stood the bent-over Indian woman. She was staring after them, her attitude strangely childlike and wistful; and he could not escape the insight that she felt cruelly forsaken, that he was leaving her behind.

Chapter 4

West and northwest of Fort Griffin, the greening country flexed itself, rising broad and endless, in long swellings of ridge chains on all sides, under the brassy shield of the hard, straight sun. By the second day traveling became easier and Martin could see the way ahead smoothing to rolling plains. Wild flowers made brilliant splashes on the matting of short, curly buffalo grass, quiltings of lavender, yellow, and red.

Eye-filling country, yet so still that it sawed on a man's nerves. Except for the phantom rushes of pronghorn antelope bands, their white rump patches bobbing, the land was as empty as a hollowed-out log, and there wasn't a sound out there; and a man, looking off, had the oppressive sensation that no life existed.

Burke stuck mostly to the wagon trail, which he explained was the main one to Rath City, on the Double Mountain Fork of the Brazos. When he took a sudden notion to leave it — and Martin was learning anew that Rip Burke had a will of his own — they came upon fields of bones whitening in the sun. Bones that layered the level stretches, visible for miles, so thick Augustin often detoured around them, for the hoofs of the mules were growing tender from the sharp trampling.

They met an incoming string of ox-drawn Studebaker wagons, huge vehicles with seven-foot-high rear wheels and bones stacked above the boxes. Painted blue, the wagons bore large block lettering in white: *R. H. HILLYARD, FORT GRIFFIN*. The first driver called out cheerfully:

"You boys better have plenty of bacon and flour. No meat to shoot around here, 'less you get an antelope or run down a jack-rabbit."

Burke spat down wind as the wagons jolted by. "Miss Ruby's boys. They know just how to water down bones 'fore they git to the railroad. Makes a load heap heavier."

81

They entered another shot-out expanse, where on both sides of the trail the glistening-white bones resembled an uprooted graveyard. Martin looked all around, hoping to sight buffalo. Nothing disturbed the cheerless distance. As heavy as he remembered the slaughter in Kansas, he recalled no desert of bones such as this, probably, he supposed, because he and Sid Trumbo had kept on the move. It all seemed long ago. Seeing a scattered skeleton every few feet or so, in a pattern, he saw again in all their clarity the patient, puzzled beasts turning in their maddening, helpless circle of death as he worked the stand. Afterward, the skinners, the wolves, the vultures. A relentless cycle. All participants in some foreordained catastrophe.

Near noon, Martin saw the first hide wagon, recognizable by its large wooden frame, built like a hay rack. Six yokes of oxen idled in front of the light load. Behind, mules pulled a cook wagon. One man rode horseback. As Augustin turned out to let the heavier vehicle pass, a strapping man whose black beard covered most of his face stared keenly at Burke and rode across.

"Rip, you old panther!" the man roared. "You sure picked the tail end of times to come out for hides."

"Didn't come to hunt," Burke said gruffly. "Just as well."

"Never liked to spring-hunt for robes, no how, when an animal's sheddin'."

"We been out since the start of grass. You can see what we got. Exactly fifty-eight hides. Buff'lo's sceerce an' wild. We're headed for home — for keeps — back to Illinois." He looked discouraged and hard-used to Martin, even for a man accustomed to the gut-busting work of hunting. He said, "Would you boys happen to have any extra coffee or tobacco? Plumb out, we are."

"We can spare some, sure," Martin said. "It's about noon. Eat with us."

The hunter's name, Martin learned, was Jess West, who said he and his two sons were quitting the business with less money than when they had started. West's eyes, blue and vigilant and friendly, showed a vague bewilderment when he talked about the buffalo.

"I don't savvy it," he said over another cup of coffee. "Buff'lo didn't go north this spring like usual. I always figured we just killed the natural increase each year. So where'd they all go, Rip?"

"You know," Burke answered, his merciless tone equally self-blaming. "We hate to admit it, is all. We killed the golden bull. We all helped."

West sighed and stood up, studied the bottom of his coffee cup a moment or two and tapped out the grounds. "I'll say this" — and he drew an air circle that included his sons and Burke — "we never took just the tongues like some outfits. Like Trumbo did at the peak. Or just shot cows because their hair was softer. Or if we shot a bull, let him rot with the hide on for the wolves. No, by God."

"We's all angels, Jess. You bet." Burke's light blue eyes, almost white against his leathery cheekbones and forehead, mocked the other hunter. "Don't matter now what we did or didn't do. Where's Trumbo, in Rath City?"

"Camped about fifteen mile down the Double Mountain Fork, last I heard," West remarked, unconcerned.

"When was that?"

"Week or so ago." West's stare hooked into Burke. "Mean you got business with *him?*"

"Hell, no. Roebuck has."

West's face settled, as if to say it was none of his affair. He tramped to his cook wagon and returned bearing an enormous smoked buffalo ham. "Leastwise," he said, giving it to Martin, "the hide game beat grubbin' stumps on a wore-out farm."

On into the afternoon the undulating land

off from Martin changed but little, as silent and vacant as though the outfit drifted on a heaving sea. Talkative springtime breezes carried the scents of sweet grasses and wild flowers, and the sharp cries of the killdeer. But his impression remained of an emerald world empty under a blue-domed sky. And in the background of his mind the reflection deepened that it was wrong to kill for the hides alone.

They were pulling up a long rise when Martin, looking behind, sighted a spot of white on the dark green swell. In a little it disappeared behind a dip in the prairie. He waited, holding his gaze on that point. After minutes he saw it again, a white dot on the wagon trail, its progress so gradual it did not seem to be moving.

Martin shouted for Augustin to hold up. Burke swung back. "We're being followed," Martin said. "Watch."

Burke looked. "Don't see a thing."

"It'll show up in a minute."

"Antelope."

"You wouldn't see a rump patch coming toward us. Tell Augustin to drive out of sight on the other side. We'll wait and see."

"You won't camp on Kioway crick tonight if you burn daylight here," Burke said.

"Wait."

85

More than half an hour wasted away. Tack rested under the wagon in the shade. Burke, still complaining over the loss of time, went to expounding to Augustin on the proper knives for skinning buffalo.

Martin rode to the crest again. The back trail stood empty, two pale, serpentine bands winding and weaving over the rich green folds. He turned toward the wagon, deciding to resume travel.

Tack stood and growled, his nose pointed down the ridge line. Martin looked.

A rider was cautiously circling in on the trail, unaware of the wagon parked higher up.

A massive astonishment took Martin as he recognized the brown mare and the old Comanche woman, still dressed in the light buckskin dress, clinging like a crab.

"Burke! Damnit! Look!"

Burke was already in the saddle, and by the time Martin loped up he could hear the two of them jabbering away in rapid-fire Comanche. Martin glared at her.

"What in God's name is she doing here? Ask her!"

Burke spoke again and cut swift signs. Her voice was halting, her signs slow. Burke, stroking his mustache, said, "Says she just got on her pony that first night. Slipped away

. . . Brought her tent 'n' everything. Says . . . she belongs to you now."

"To me!" Martin exploded.

"Says you saved her life. Gave her food. Gave her a little tent. A good pony. Didn't let the pony soldiers kill her . . . She ain't much, she says. She's old. Her eyes are dim. But she can cook meat good. Make fires. She knows the country."

Martin slumped in disgust. Still, when he noticed how thin and wrinkled and exhausted she looked, and how the smoky-brown eyes hung on his every reaction, apprehensive of what he might do, he felt himself weaken. A thought spun: she was addled. A little crazy. But when he saw the proud face, and the clarity in the old eyes, and the faint, lost smile, all on the verge of pleading and yet not, he wasn't certain.

She had, he saw, fashioned a crude saddle from one of the blankets he had given her, and secured it around the mare's belly with a leather strap. Another blanket, slung across the animal's withers, apparently held her belongings, including the tent. A piece of rope, looped just above the mare's nose, served as a bridle. A butcher knife, no doubt stolen from Harriet Sanford's kitchen, was thrust inside her rope belt. She stuck to the makeshift saddle like a clump of moss, all humped over and wizened, breathing through her mouth, stubbornly resisting her evident weariness.

"She's got a name for you," Burke went on.

"A name?" Martin said resentfully. And was Burke grinning behind his crusty beard?

"Yep. Your Comanche name is His-Heart-Is-Good — Good Heart, for short . . . She says Tehannas killed her last son five summers ago on a raid. Now you're like a son to her. Her heart is off the ground. Her spirit is strong again. She's here to protect you . . . Says there's heap bad white men on the plains. Some bad Injuns, too. She's got powers."

Martin snorted.

"She's a medicine woman, she says. Recollect what I told you at Griffin? So if you want to hunt buff'lo, she says she can find some." The ghost of a smile flitted back across his face. "She shore has taken a shine to you, Roebuck."

Martin pinched in his lips. His mind was running ahead, seeing how she would burden and slow the outfit. He reined to go.

"What about her?"

"She'll just have to travel along."

"With us?"

"Who else?"

Before fawn twilight caught them they camped on Kiowa Creek, which was more branch than creek, and offered water only because this was springtime and not summer. The old woman watered the mare and rode to a mesquite, slid crab-like to the ground, took off her blanket roll and saddle and struggled to put up the tent.

Martin withstood the wish to help her. Hereafter, he told himself, she had to shift for herself and quit depending on Augustin and him. The simplest solution was for her to return to her people. There was no other way, despite what Burke said about Comanche superstition. And thus Martin foresaw that her presence, hindering as it was, could supply the answer after all. Because here she was closer to her tribesmen than she had been at Griffin. From out here she could find them again.

Augustin cooked supper over a buffalo-chip fire, and afterward the men grouped around the wagon to smoke and talk. A coolness rose over the prairie. Martin knew they were gradually climbing as they traveled toward Double Mountain and the Cap Rock. Always the air felt fresh, even in the heat of high noon. It made the blood race and instilled in a man the notion that he was bigger than his shadow.

Burke slipped off to his bedroll and back, bringing the pungent taint of barroom whisky. He grew garrulous. Yet his cantankerous side seemed to fall away and, in place, Martin discerned something of the naturalness of the man.

"I recollect on the Sweet Water when I shot my first silk," Burke began. "Why, it was like a panful o' gold. Fifty dollars I got for it in Fort Griffin. It took Ruby Hillyard's eye — Miss Ruby herself." He laughed and continued, "Though I reckon she doubled her money somewhere. In my time, I calculate all told I shot ten silks or more."

"Silks?" Augustin sounded puzzled.

"Slickest buff'lo robes you ever saw. Soft as silk. Dark. Almost always from a cow. A peculiar shine to 'em. I always held out a silk — sold it separate. Man should take robes only in the fall, when the buff'lo's put on his new brown coat for winter." He slapped his thigh. "I God, that's the time, boys!"

Burke talked on, chiefly for the benefit of the avid Augustin, who had never hunted buffalo. He calculated, Burke said, that for every hide taken to market, one or two were lost on the range. Some inexperienced hunters failed to poison the hides in the summer and the hide bugs ruined them. Badly wounded animals walked off to die in ravines and thickets; other perished in bogs. Some died of thirst when the hide outfits, camped around watering holes, bombarded them daily and the shaggies couldn't drink.

"Most of us whooped off what we made," Burke concluded. "What didn't go to Griffin's skinflint storekeepers for supplies. Some big outfits made money, though. Good money . . . Little odd, too. Seems they didn't shoot all the hides they hauled to market."

"Wagon tracks are plain for several days in short-grass country," Martin said. "It's not hard to trail thieves."

"Nope," Burke agreed in a dry voice, "if you want to git your butt shot off. Got worse last year, when we first knew game was thin an' prices went up."

"You talk like it's about over," Martin said.

"Ain't it — goddamnit to hell? Ain't it? Didn't we all gut the country? Didn't we? I reckon Buffalo Burke knows when a thing's played out."

Burke was staring off. In his reminiscent mood, he seemed to have forgotten that others sat nearby. There was a farness in his manner, a going back, Martin thought, which was an old man's special province, with an old man's special sadness, as he ached for youth and the lusty good times of the vanished past.

All at once Burke turned his head. Martin followed his gaze, sensing company before he saw it.

The old Comanche woman stood a few feet away, ghostly in her pale buckskins in the gloom. Martin suspected that she had been there some time, waiting to be seen and relishing that the hated whites hadn't noticed her. He was conscience of her approving gaze. In the claws of her hands she clutched a small object as a child might an offering.

She took a hopeful step toward him, another, another, and became unsure. She stopped and held out her right hand, the palm open. Martin saw a piece of bone or stone, three or four inches long. He did not take it. She tendered the offering again.

"What is it?" he said, leaning back.

Burke spoke in Comanche. Her high voice replied in a tone new to Martin.

"Mary," Burke said, and it annoyed Martin that the hunter insisted on using the name, "wants you to take the bone. It's medicine bone — from the cannibal owl." Martin stayed motionless. Burke spoke louder: "It's part of her power. Her medicine. She wants to protect you. Says it'll draw out poison from a bad wound, ease a man's pain. Cure 'bout anything. It's a present, Roebuck." In the sooty light,

Burke's askew mouth fashioned a rougish amusement.

Deciding to humor her so she would leave, Martin stood and extended his hand and felt her press the piece of bone into his palm, felt it grow clammy against his skin. She nodded in approbation and continued to face him, her black eyes favoring him, a warm and steady light in them, until Martin shifted his feet. She spoke softly once, turned and wobbled away.

"Now what did all that mean?" Martin asked.

Burke's laugh was half-grunt. "She called you her white son."

Martin started to pitch the bone aside. And then, turning his body, yielding to a vague impulse he didn't understand, he drew his hand back and, covertly, dropped it into his coat pocket.

It happened late in the afternoon of the fourth day, off the wagon road in a knuckle of green hills where a silvery spring formed a bright pool and ran shimmering down a wooded draw. Buffalo wallows ringed the grassy flat.

Martin saw the white down of bones, in greater density because of the watering places, also as somehow vernal, partly obscured among the patches of vivid wild flowers struggling, it seemed, to cover the shame of the ravaged plain.

Tack growled. The coarse, black hair on the dog's back lifted and he bared his teeth, a wolf in that alertness.

A shaggy white man was traveling up the draw astride a poor gelding. He rode within the camp's edge, pulled up, hunched forward, left elbow on the saddle horn, and inclined his head in greeting. Another rider followed, and a second, and they halted on a line, spaced out, an interval between them, each contemplating by turn the stout wagon, the cooking utensils, the tents, the picketed mules and the saddle horses, each man giving the semblance of marking everything down in his mind. Behind them in the draw one rider herded pack mules.

To Martin the riders all looked spawned from the identical nondescript stamp, bearded, long-jawed, lank, greasy-eyed, and dark with grime. The first man was older, the father or uncle of the others. All had rifles in long saddle boots and an assortment of knives stuck inside their belts.

A hackling sensation swept over Martin as he thought of his six-shooter in the wagon. Augustin, busy cooking when the three rode in, was also unarmed. Burke wasn't in sight.

The Indian woman watched outside her tent.

" 'Pears like you-ins sorter nabbed the best campin' place," the older rider said.

"We got here first," Martin said.

The other pondered the camp's contents again. Speculation burned openly in his eyes. "Best water, too."

"Plenty room and water down the draw."

"Not like hereabouts. Figured we'd camp closeby. Be neighborly."

Martin held on to his temper, knowing there wasn't time to take the few steps to the wagon and grab the revolver behind the tailgate. And where the hell was Burke? He heard the rider speak again:

"I said we'd be neighborly."

"Suit yourself," Martin said, voicing an indifference not in him.

Tack barked suddenly as the man started his horse drifting in. The rider checked and an infuriating calculation coiled across his sharp features. "Wouldn't he make a nice pelt, boys?"

"Let the dog alone," Martin said. "He won't bother you unless I say so."

"Smart 'un, is he?" The voice conveyed contempt.

Then the horseman on Martin's left, whose greasy locks hung down like a woebegone sheep dog, sent his gaunt beast approaching the wagon's rear. Tack tensed. Martin spoke sharply and the big mongrel held, though trembling, his hair on edge. The rider came on.

"Stay away from the wagon," Martin told him, and took two steps nearer the tailgate. The rider drew his horse in and dropped his hand to the pommel, slid it downward to the rifle boot and gripped hard on the rifle butt, the knobs of his knuckles showing white. He darted a look at the older man for orders.

Martin stood still. He turned his eyes, seeing Augustin standing by the buffalo-chip fire, clenching a spoon, as helpless as himself.

A gruff voice called, "Hold it right there —" It was Burke's, finally. Martin let out his breath, conscious of an extraordinary relief.

Caught off guard, the riders froze and stared across the draw.

Martin stepped quickly to the wagon and spun around with the handgun. A slouch hat in the green thicket by the spring gave Burke's location. He came into the open, holding the Ballard on the riders. Martin noticed a spring in his step as he walked across, talking as he did:

"If it ain't the Claxtons an' good old Uncle Mose. Might 'a' knowed. Hit the grit.

You're smellin' up our camp."

"Jest tryin' to be neighborly," Mose Claxton said, innocent-faced.

"Clean us out — you mean. Naw — you don't camp near us."

Mose Claxton roved hungry eyes once more over the camp and turned his horse and the rest followed single file. After a short distance, he flung about and called, "Hit's got so a man can't earn his salt out here. I've took my last pelt for any damned skinflint female!"

"Wolfers," Burke branded them scornfully as the Claxtons went on. "Meanest, thievingest breed on the plains. They slink along after the hide outfits. Don't seem to mind the stench 'n' flies." A withering disdain filled his face. "Poison ever' buff'lo carcass for miles — strychnine. Wolf or coyote comes up, gorges himself; in a bit he dies in agony. Times are bad when scavengers like the Claxtons haul their freight."

"He said he sold pelts to a woman. Did he mean . . . ?"

Burke's sneer was knowing. "Who d'you think? Wolf hides bring two-bits to fifty cents in Griffin at the big store."

"I see," said Martin, not surprised. Wasn't it all cold business? Any sport hunting buffalo had ceased long ago. The wolfers must be after his time on the plains; he didn't recall any in Kansas. With them the slaughter took on new dimensions: first the bands of hunters, the real destroyers, himself among them; followed by the furtive wolfers, and finally the bone-pickers driving their big blue wagons, each wave living off ruination.

After supper, Martin and Burke saddled up and located the Claxtons camped a mile or so down the meandering spring-fed draw. That night they decided to picket the stock close by the wagon and to take turns standing guard. Augustin the first watch, next Burke and Martin.

The night was still and cool as Martin took his turn. He made a circling round of the camp and returned to the wagon, watching the star-glitter, his mind reaching ahead. What would it be like facing Trumbo after so long? It was easy to imagine the disarming greeting, the noisy heartiness. The surface things. It was in other ways that a man really changed. Ways you couldn't see or hear, more sensed than evident.

He didn't know when the strangeness started or when he discovered it. Something low and murmurous. A humming. A vibration. A *m-mm-mmm-um-mm*. It brought a singular sensation and it seemed to reach him over a great distance, as though he could glimpse the whole breadth of his life across the mystery of space and through the incredible emptiness of the once-teeming buffalo country. Which possibly was the only reason he could hear it at all, because of the emptiness, whatever it was or whatever it meant.

Daylight charged over the sparkling prairie, peeling away the dimness, and the sound vanished with the light, like a spent echo fading away, a mere whisper, until Martin doubted that he had even heard it.

He yawned and looked off, and started up at the crack of a rifle. More shots, a quick spattering. Everything came from the south, down the draw. He began to read a meaning in the shooting. Not the booming of buffalo rifles. These shots sounded lighter.

Burke and Augustin were up and watching, the Frenchman clutching his shotgun. The morning fell still.

"No buff'lo hereabouts," Burke said, crotchety and stubborn, sniffing the wind. "I God," he said after a minute, "I smell smoke," and froze.

Martin saw, too. Horsemen moving up the draw, too far away yet to tell much about them. He could think only of the Claxtons, except there were too many dark shapes approaching to be the wolfers. As the horsemen trotted higher up the draw, the pale light caught them and, of a sudden, laid greasy glimmers on half-naked bronze bodies.

Burke swore and broke for his picketed horse. Augustin, who had never seen a war party, stood transfixed, his face pale.

Martin's shout shook Augustin out of his trance, and Martin, striding for his own mount, noticed the Indian woman standing by her tent and squinting south. He motioned her to get into the wagon, but she continued to stand there watching. He hurried on.

With the stock tied behind the wagon, Martin faced the draw again and saw the Indians halt about three-hundred yards away. Fifteen or twenty bucks, he judged, and as the light strengthened he could see smoke rising above the wolfers' camp.

The Indians jogged on a piece and spread out, appearing to study the camp by the spring. Well out of range behind them Martin saw a little huddle of people and horses dragging travois poles.

"They're on the move," Burke said. "Got their women an' kids along."

Martin took a sack of shells and the Sharps from its case, opened it by yanking down on the big trigger guard and slipped in a long cartridge. After some four years, the heavy-barreled rifle felt awkward in his hands.

"Let's see you dust off some tail feathers," Burke said. "My old Ballard ain't the hoss it was once."

Martin steadied his elbows on the tailgate, lined up and barely squeezed the trigger and felt the butt kick his shoulder. At the solid boom a pony toppled. The Indians scattered. Martin worked the lever and reloaded.

Burke was sneering. "Point blank range for a Sharps — you knock down a pony."

"I *was* shooting at the pony. Now they know we outrange 'em, maybe they won't rush us."

Burke snorted his dissent to such strategy and brought up the Ballard, watching.

A horse clattered around the wagon from behind, and Martin's eyes widened on the old woman. She heaped scolding Comanche upon him, shaking her head in excitement, bringing her right hand up and down, dropping it in the pushing sign for Wait. She repeated the sign until Martin lowered the Sharps.

Her wiveled features favored him a crinkling smile of approval, her black eyes shone. And, slapping reins across the mare's withers, she loped down the draw.

"What she do?" Augustin asked.

"I think," Martin said, "she's going back to her people."

"Don't bet on it," Burke grumbled.

At her determined appearance, some of the scattering Indians checked their flight, and by the time she reached the dead pony, most of them were swung around watching her. She halted by the pony and motioned them in.

Several edged cautiously back, careful not to bunch up. Others rode toward her. Suddenly everyone came in faster.

They were within feet of the tiny, humped figure when, without warning, they wheeled frantically and dashed quirting away, yelling, in disorder.

She watched them punish their ponies and splash across the branch and out of the shallow draw, and when they reached the level prairie, she turned around and rode for camp.

Martin felt the last of his expectancy die. They couldn't be her people.

He noticed the change in her while she walked the gentle mare toward them. In this brief time, she looked smaller and more shrunken. All her animation gone. Looking much as she did the first day, terribly weary.

She spoke to Burke in sparse, toneless words.

"They're Kwahadi," he said. "Hungry an' mean. On the lookout west for buff'lo."

"They'd run from an old woman?" But a perception disturbed Martin as he scoffed, and he saw it strengthen in Burke's bright stare.

"They're part of her band," Burke said. "That's why they spooked. They saw the ghost of the old medicine woman they left to die way north of Griffin."

Martin accepted that now and more. "We've got her on our hands hereon. But I can't forget how she rode out there and saved our hides. She didn't have to, did she?"

Chapter 5

Noon sun was punishing them before they finished the dismal task of burying the wolfers, and when time came to go, Martin, observing the old woman's exhaustion, helped her into the wagon on a pallet. She did not protest. Neither did she give any sign that she cared what he did with her, not until he turned away, whereupon the old eyes, almost shuttered, opened and rested on his face, faintly glowing.

Repelled, Martin went quickly to his horse.

Uncomplaining, she rode all that day and through the next. On the third morning she looked noticeably stronger. At noon she saddled the mare and followed the wagon. On the fourth day she mounted when Burke and Martin did and took her place.

Her improvement baffled Martin. He decided it wasn't the rest from riding horseback; a jolting ride in Augustin's wagon was as tiring. Could it be because they were coming closer to the buffalo? Illogical as that seemed, it clung to his mind, more feeling than reason. She held her head high, and when he looked back, she was ever squinting to the northwest, a grimace of anticipation scrawled over her myriad of wrinkles.

As the wagon trailed on toward the Double Mountain Fork of the Brazos, Martin was never out of sight of buffalo bones, and never in sight of a live buffalo. Unthinkable, for here stretched the range of the great southern herd, where the army of hunters has descended after exterminating the shaggies in eastern Colorado, western Kansas, and in the Platte, Solomon, and Republican rivers country.

Riding up the gradual rises of short-grassed prairie, he often sensed within himself the wish to find buffalo darkening the next broad sweep of land. But his eyes saw only the ruin of where they had fallen, and that some time ago, shown by carcasses picked so bare they no longer attracted wolves and vultures. Now and then the surrounding litter created fleeting images in his mind, and he groped for suitable descriptions. At the moment he thought of great snowflakes fallen in vast profusion, banked in shallow drifts where conditions — the hunter's undetected approach, the wind to his face, the lassitude of a quiet day, the unsuspecting animals — had combined to bring about the slaughter of a stand.

He used to hear hunters around campfires call the buffalo the most stupid game animal in the world; surprisingly, more than a few argued the point. He remembered himself asking: Was a defenseless wild thing, supreme in its own environment, supposed to have the brain of man? Wasn't man responsible to nature because he was wiser?

He remembered the laughs as well, Trumbo's among them, as the jug was passed.

He was glad when the first deep booms rolled out of the northwest, from the valley of the Double Mountain Fork, welcoming sounds which meant life still survived.

Burke turned and grinned, unusual for him when regarding Martin; and the Comanche, riding up as they halted, released a gabbling excitement on Burke.

"Mary says she wishes we'd shoot a fat

buff'lo cow for her. She's hungry for raw liver."

Miles away, rising out of the plains across the deceptive distance, stood the stubs of landmark mountains.

"Double Mountain," Burke said, speaking with familiarity. "From here it looks like two mountains. Work around to the north, looks like three mountains, sometimes. Keep on west an' look back to the southeast, looks like two again. They'll fool you after sundown. Reckon it's the shadows."

They moved on. Around Martin the heads of the carcasses began to show black hair and chin-mops, and farther on vultures sailed and dived across the sky.

Suddenly, he lowered his head against a terrible stench and pressed his nose. Nausea clutched his stomach. He recoiled as though from a blow. The stink was like a stain upon the clear air, real enough to be tangible to the touch. A revulsion you had to get used to, he remembered over again, although you never did completely.

And soon afterward the bloated greenhead flies started swarming, pestering the horses and mules and making them miserable.

Burke led down to the fork and turned up it, in the direction of the shooting, which slackened and quit. He followed the stream for a couple of miles. Without notice, he stopped and pointed to tents and wagons on a mesquite flat back from the fork.

"Far as I go," he stated, and suddenly his old belligerence rang in his voice. "I'll take my pay now, Roebuck. There's Trumbo's camp."

Martin overcame his astonishment. "You quit? What's wrong?"

"Aim to have myself a spree in Rath."

"Thought you hired on for the whole trip, out and back?"

"Agreed to find Trumbo's camp," Burke said stubbornly. "That's all."

That wasn't all, Martin knew. And Burke's continual crabbedness, his unwarned leave-taking, his high independence — everything was swiftly too much for Martin, and he swerved to the wagon for the money and rushed back and counted it out.

"That's for ten days — a hundred dollars," he said. "Now, something's been stuck in your craw from the minute you hired on. What the hell is it?"

A choleric retort swelled Burke's jowls and brought flint point to his light blue eyes. He rammed the greenbacks inside his greasy shirt and swiped the back of his left hand slant-ways across his stubbly chin, fixing a curious intentness on Martin. Something restrained him and Martin saw him shed his perversity by loath degrees and become the Buffalo Burke of the Planters' House, wolfing down a gift breakfast that would have strained the capacity of a man twice his size, while pre-empting the role of the host, and complaining loudly over money, and by turns foxy and guileless, one moment preenishly proud and the next affecting humility.

"Wouldn't come a-tall if I hadn't felt plumb sorry for your green pilgrim outfit," Burke confessed; for the old man, in his excessive vanity, Martin saw now, had never accepted him on equal terms as another buffalo hunter. "So long, Roebuck."

Burke spurred off up the ford, arms flapping, and shortly his voice floated back to Martin in tuneless anticipation:

"Oh, 'twas in the town of Jacksboro, in the spring of seventy-three . . ."

Mesquite smoke, escaping in stringy tendrils over the valley, scented the hot afternoon as Martin came near the camp, a far larger outfit than he had expected. Altogether a dozen tents and wagons. Black mounds of stacked hides, a virtual hide yard, and a few hides pegged out to dry, flesh sides up; ammunition boxes, tin cans, coffee pots, kettles, Dutch ovens, kegs, and a clutter of straight-bladed knives for ripping and curved ones for skinning. Buffalo tongues hung like black pelts from a rough pole framework; underneath a fire was smoldering, its smoke serving the additional purpose of discouraging the hordes of fires. A mighty stink pervaded here as well.

A man rose from a grindstone, holding the long-bladed knife he had been sharpening. He tallied to a general type found on the buffalo range: rough, bearded, slouch hat, only dirtier than most. Could be skinner, driver, or handyman. No hunter, Martin discerned. At any rate not an old-type hunter — buffalo runners, as they called themselves, men with pride. Martin rode around a stack of hides and spoke to the man, who stared back in silence. At the same time another man poked his head out a tent door and a third stepped around a wagon. A feeling bored into Martin from the flank, and he found still a fourth man, rifle cradled, posted by a hide stack.

"Hello," Martin said again to the one with the knife. "This Sid Trumbo's camp?"

"What d'you want?" The words leaked from the corners of the bearded mouth. He drew a whetstone from his hip pocket and in an absent manner, yet conspicuously, began to hone the straight blade. A special blade, Martin saw, because of its bone handle. Back and forth the man passed the blade over the stone, raising a gritty rasping.

"Want to see Trumbo."

"He ain't around."

The three men in front of Martin were busy eyeing his wagon, halted well back out of the camp's stink, and which appeared to allay their suspicions.

"Expect him soon?" Martin asked.

"Hard to tell."

Martin sat still, watching the surly faces, and a feeling rolled over him, maybe sprung from those early years, that secretly he had expected a reception like this. Once more he went on:

"Maybe later today? Tomorrow?"

The man shrugged. But before Martin could speak again, a voice called, "It's all right, Coley," a hearty voice which he recognized at once. Then he turned and saw Sid Trumbo filling the doorway of a big blue wagon made into a house on wheels, steps leading up and a black chimney rising from the canvas top.

"Sid!" Martin said.

Trumbo took the steps in three's, calling, "Martin — Martin! Get down, man!" and he was there as Martin dismounted, swinging his right arm in a vast arc and gripping Martin's hand and pounding Martin's shoulder over and over.

Almost against his will, Martin felt himself responding to the greeting, because, in a way, he was glad to see Sid Trumbo again; it was hard not to like the man. At first glance, Trumbo looked unchanged. Straight and large of bone, about thirty now, two years older than Martin, he had the same bold and impatient face, except the appealing suggestion of boyish sensitivity that Martin remembered was missing.

"Well, Sid, how've you been?"

"Seen better prospects in the middle of a Kansas blizzard," Trumbo replied, smiling as only he could, shaking his disheveled yellow head, and Martin saw the flash of the man that used to take hold of people, men as well as women. The grayish-blue eyes kindling the promise of excitement and fortune, the brown skin, smooth shaven in a land of predominantly thicket-bearded men, and the strong, even teeth, set whitely in the wide and sensuous mouth.

Only now the eyes looked moody, instead, and he wore a growth on his face of days, and he was putting on tallow at the waist and chest, and his face looked bloated.

Grease stained the front of his unbuttoned flannel shirt, which recalled for Martin how Trumbo liked to wear it open to show the curly hair matting his wide chest. Trumbo's Wellington boots, whose glossiness he had guarded in the old days, also betrayed neglect.

Martin glanced casually over the rows of hide stacks. "Looks profitable enough."

"Bulk of these hides been here for months," Trumbo said, his head-shake discounting. "Haven't hauled out yet. All we're doing now is cleaning out little bunches of buff across the river. The plush days you and I used to know are gone, Martin. That's for sure."

To the apparent truth of the last Martin admitted. However, he sensed a play on hard times in preparation for the business still to come.

"Let's have a reunion drink," Trumbo said and slapped Martin across the back.

Martin, nodding to that, accompanied him to the wagon. Inside was a world apart after the littered camp. Trumbo's fetish for the comforts of life hadn't changed. On the unmade bed were sheets and pillows in cases. A bowl and pitcher occupied a commode top. And Martin noted further a clothes press, wood-burning stove, and a writing desk holding bottles, coal-oil lamp, and a confusion of papers. Two Sharps rifles stood in a walnut gun rack. The canvas ceiling let in a fallow light which created a still greater detachment from the stink and grime outside.

Trumbo stepped to the desk, poured two glasses of whisky, handed one to Martin and, lifting his glass, murmured:

"Here's to old times."

Martin, meeting his eyes, downed his drink. The whisky was hot and raw. Seeing the first uneasiness in Trumbo, he decided to let it grow.

"Guess I know why you're here," Trumbo said after a bit. A rueful expression, still one that evoked sympathy, skipped across his face.

"Five thousand dollars is a heap of money right now," Martin told him. "Two years ago you wrote me. Asked me to back you. Prospects looked good, you said. We'd be partners. You'd run several outfits. So for old times' sake I gathered up the money; borrowed part of it. It all sounded good. Remember?"

"I remember." A slackness dulled Trumbo's voice. "Didn't expect you till next fall."

"Changed my mind," Martin said, speaking evenly. "I want an accounting, Sid. That's only fair and square. You haven't paid a dime in over a year, and I know you've been hunting. You've got men out now, today. I heard shooting as I rode in. Prices are higher than they've ever been. Why'd you pass me by?"

Trumbo poured himself another drink. His confidence returned. "I can explain everything."

"Let's see," Martin said, studying the contents of his glass. "Last spring you wrote me that Comanches burned you out — everything. A season's kill, you said. Last fall . . . I forgot what it was you said."

"Goddamnit" — Trumbo made a wrenching motion — "it was the truth. And what if I don't have the money?"

"Plenty of hides in camp. Prices are up."

"What you saw out there isn't all mine. Couple other hunters headquarter here."

"Not all *yours?*" Martin said.

"Well, *ours,* Goddamnit. *Ours.* Hell, if you don't trust an old friend more'n that, how'd you even know I'd be in Texas?"

"Because," Martin said, "you'll never hunt Wyoming or Montana. You can't take the rugged winters." A weariness was settling over him, and a self-rebuke for having traveled so far to find no more than this. Trumbo was dodging and he'd continue to dodge. Now he saw Trumbo curb his temper and, apparently, fall into a reminiscing mood.

"I was thinking," the big man said, "how long it's been since we had a drink together. Not since Angie died. Just before you quit chasing buff."

Pain twisted in Martin, deep-running, and then it changed to resentment that Trumbo should use her name as a means of evasion.

"That was over four years ago," Martin said. "And it has nothing to do with the fact that you owe the money."

"Oh, I think it does, Martin. It sure as hell does. Why'd you back me in the first place?" Both were standing, each gripping his glass. It was Martin who looked away first, seeing a reminder in Trumbo's glare.

Martin said, "I haven't forgotten you saved my life that time in Dodge, in that crazy saloon brawl we got into. You shot a man for me, Sid. And, too, Angie liked you. Yes, she did. That was enough for me. So . . ."

Trumbo's head lifted up and down, a slight movement of acknowledgment, almost unseen to the eye, which nevertheless Martin saw and understood, and which flushed chafing heat to his face because Trumbo expected him to remember an old debt.

Trumbo idled to the open door and looked out.

"You knew you were taking a chance when you went in with me," he said, talking over his shoulder. "Chasing buff is a risky game." He stepped back to the desk, sloshed his glass full and sat down heavily. "Like I said, I can explain if you'll listen."

"Shoot."

"Like I wrote you, last spring I had a winter's kill ready for market. I was on the Salt Fork. Comanches burned me out, killed two skinners and the cook . . . Last fall, at Rath City, I sold to Jim Hickey, an agent for W. C. Lobenstein of Leavenworth."

"How many hides?"

"I remember exactly — three thousand, two hundred and fifty-one."

"How much?"

"I made a good deal. Three dollars apiece. All prime robes. Not a kip hide in the lot." Martin saw his sudden ranking. "If you don't believe me, you can look in my memorandum book."

"All right," Martin said.

Trumbo pawed through the papers and handed Martin a small black book. "It's right there — on November 17."

Martin found the entry. Everything was as

Trumbo had said. "That's not the point," he said, skepticism rising in his voice. "What happened to the money?"

"Paid the crew, went on a spree — got robbed of every cent." Disgust shaped along his mouth. He looked down. It was, Martin had to admit, a disarming and penitent performance.

"How did it happen?"

"Simple. Somebody stuck a gun in my back."

"Why didn't you tell me?" Martin asked, unconvinced.

"Would you've believed me after what happened in the spring?"

"Guess not." Martin set his glass on the desk. "Tell you what, though, Sid. I'd been a damned sight more ready to if you'd just told you'd blown it all on some girls in Fort Worth."

Trumbo stood suddenly. He was smiling again and shaking his head from side to side. "See what I mean, man? You wouldn't have. Nobody would. So I didn't give another excuse . . . Well, I'm making it all back, Martin, I sure as hell am — and I will. You bet! Before long I'll lay at least a thousand dollars in your hands."

"That's a start," Martin said, unappeased and sensing delay. "When?" Glancing through the doorway, he could see Trumbo's men lounging within easy earshot of the wagon. An uneasiness grazed him, then passed as Trumbo spoke:

"Oh . . . in a week or two. We'll haul in soon as we finish off these little bunches."

Martin went to the door, saw the heads turn and look away when they saw who it was. His nerves were tingling. At that instant he thought of old Rip Burke standing in the thicket by the spring, his scrap-metal carbin ready in his thorny hands.

"Don't mind waiting a little longer for your money, do you, Martin?" Trumbo said.

"We can use the rest."

"Another drink?"

Martin declined, adding that he would look for a camping place.

"There's a good spot about a hundred yards up from us," Trumbo volunteered. "You'll be out of the stink a little more. I'll bring some meat over for your supper . . . In a day or so we'll go hunting. Be like old times."

"Yeah," Martin said, starting down the steps. "Like old times."

Leaving the smelly camp Martin felt a marked relief to be placing it behind him. Several things puzzled him. Why wasn't Trumbo, a crack shot whom he had seen kill a buffalo bull with one slug from a Sharps .40-90 at four hundred yards, out hunting? Trumbo looked dissipated, way out of condition, indicating a long absence from the buffalo range. And the story about being robbed? That, Martin couldn't believe. Sid Trumbo just wasn't the careless sort who let himself be taken off guard, drunk or sober. By a woman, possibly, though she would regret it later; by a man, never. As for Trumbo's play of letting Martin see the memorandum book, in which every hunter kept count of the day's kill and all business transactions, that meant little. Anybody could make tracks match on paper. Where it all went was what mattered.

After watering the stock and setting up camp, a good deal of the afternoon remained. Idle, Martin saw how irksome the delay was going to be for him. And he wondered, then, if he shouldn't have crowded Trumbo harder for the money. But how? One man against the whole camp?

The depressive stillness of the country bothered him again. That was when he realized the surly booming had ceased, in fact, quite a while ago.

He studied the outflung camp, still curious over its size, its air of indolence in a back-breaking trade, its guarded suspicion among a breed of men noted for open friendliness. He liked none of it, yet he couldn't unravel it.

At length he saw Trumbo riding out on a temperish, buckskin gelding, a lumpy sack slung across his saddle, and upon him the heaviness of a man who hadn't pounded leather in a long time.

Trumbo waved, then Martin, and the awareness came to him that each had hesitated. He could see Trumbo's broad grin. He was shaved and he wore a clean shirt and his Wellingtons shone. Same old Sid, Martin thought. Just like he used to be.

But as Trumbo rode closer and closer, Martin's impression retreated and the image he saw was different, broken abruptly when Trumbo called out, "Smoked tongues —" and pitched the sack at Martin.

It was an elusive thing Martin sensed. In the way Trumbo did it. Not really giving. Martin held the sack without speaking.

Trumbo stepped down and surveyed the camp. Tack was growling beside the wagon. His hackles were up. Martin silenced him harshly, sharper than he intended.

"What a monster!" Trumbo exclaimed. "I can see he's not on my side. Keep him close to camp, else my men will shoot him for a wolf."

"He never bothers anybody. Do me a

favor, Sid. Pass word around camp so they'll look out for him."

"Sure. Sure."

When Martin showed Augustin the tongues, the Frenchman's black eyes became lively and he jogged his head in appreciation to Trumbo, chattering his thanks.

"A Frenchy?" Trumbo observed as Martin returned.

"Best cook on the plains," Martin said, not expecting to have to defend Augustin as he just had Tack. "I can offer you some brandy."

Afterward, talking and drinking, they turned to the other end of the wagon, in the direction of the stream. Not far away rose the shelter tent. The mare grazed almost against it, Martin saw, as closeby as the old woman could picket her for company.

Trumbo stared curiously. His mouth fell when the Comanche appeared in the opening. She crawled out, with effort swayed to her feet and went feebly toward the stream, carrying a small wooden bucket which Augustin had given her.

"She's with you?" Trumbo asked, dumbfounded.

Martin shortened the telling, only mentioning Harriet Sanford's role and leaving out the old woman's absurd adoption of him as her son. "She's very old," Martin concluded, "and probably doesn't have long to live. We're sort of looking out for her by force of circumstances, which is damned small payment after the way she scared off that war party."

"War party?" When Martin explained, Trumbo said, "You haven't changed any. Reminds me of when you took in Angie."

Trumbo's tone, while reminiscent, caused Martin to look at him. A constant edginess stirred in the man. A belittling, which though faint, lay always beneath the surface of Trumbo's conversation; and a throwing out of veiled innuendoes, of disparaging references to the old times, which, Martin knew, had been the best days of their lives.

"Isn't your memory a little rusty, Sid? I never took Angie in. I looked out for her a little — you did, too. She never asked for help. She was stranded in Dodge. She was waiting for the brother who never turned up."

"That's what she told us," Trumbo said, but he directed his meaning scrupulously down the middle.

"She *did have* a brother," Martin insisted. "Worked on the Santa Fe. He was killed at Granada. An accident. You knew that."

"I don't remember."

"Wish now," Martin said, "we'd gone ahead — been married. Not waited. It was my idea to hold off. I didn't think a hide camp was any place for a woman. She didn't last long after she got pneumonia."

"Maybe there was another reason."

"On my part?"

"No — hers."

Martin cut him a look. "I don't get all this, Sid. What's behind the bush?"

"Look, man." Trumbo spread his hands in a gesture of well-meaning reluctance. "It's just something I heard around the saloons. I never told you, of course, knowing how you felt about her."

"Just what?"

"Well — only . . ." Trumbo shook his head.

"Speak up!"

"Well . . . that she wasn't good enough for an honest man. Something about before she met you."

There was a tearing loose inside Martin. He wasn't afraid of Trumbo. He stepped across, and Trumbo stepped back, a hasty apology forming on his lips. "Sorry I ever told you now. I'm not saying it's true."

Martin didn't let up. "Then why bring it up at all? She's gone."

"Figured you ought to know. So you wouldn't go on feeling you'd lost something that . . . that maybe never existed." He turned on his broad smile. "Hell of a time to argue, just when old friends meet again. Man, let's go hunting tomorrow."

"Too soon for me."

"Come on. We'll have some fun. Like the old days."

Martin held back, feeling no enthusiasm. Then he thought of the interlude until Trumbo broke camp, of the flies and the stink around here. For the first time Trumbo seemed like his old self, persuasive, obliging, all trace of his roundabout remarks erased. At least the hunt would break the boredom of waiting.

"What about day after tomorrow?" Martin asked.

"Suits me fine."

About dark a hide wagon crossed the ford from the northwest and crawled into Trumbo's camp and stopped. Martin glanced up, then resumed cleaning his Sharps rifle by lantern light.

Chapter 6

Before daylight Martin heard a wagon creaking away from Trumbo's camp toward the hunting grounds. By nine o'clock the prospects of waiting idly throughout the day became tedious; henceforth, taking a light rifle, he set out on horseback across the Double Mountain Fork.

In his ears sounded a remote booming, which he reckoned as toward Double Mountain, northwest, and the infrequency of the shooting as the work of a solitary hunter. During an hour's leisurely ride to the north, just looking, the firing spent itself, a fading that didn't surprise him in view of the littered void through which he rode, and the stench he sought to escape by spurring to reach the wind-swept ridges. And when he rode upon the high places, the dreary emptiness stretched on and on as far as he could force his eyes, an unending dark, green herbage, sprinkled white, offering a succulence virtually uncropped this spring.

The single hunter strayed in and out of his thinking. A man couldn't make expenses on returns that poor. Not after you bought wagons and teams and good saddle horses, bedrolls, tents, cooking utensils, provisions, and Sharps or Remington rifles. Dupont and Hazard powder was high, but English powder — Curtis & Harvey's — ran half again as much and was worth every grain. Not after you paid skinners two-bits a hide, or if a five- or six-man outfit shared equally after deducting expenses. You had to knock down a quota of twenty-five shaggies a day to make money, counting the good days when you killed fifty or sixty, about all a small outfit could handle, and the days when you didn't scratch, when the wind shifted and suddenly the buffalo vanished, as if some mysterious force of nature commanded them.

Why, then, was Trumbo lingering in shot-out country that plainly couldn't support a one-wagon outfit? Where were the little bunches he kept talking about?

Northwest, timber scrawled the dark outline of a struggling creek, and farther on a lone peak, rocky and broken, suggested the ruins of a medieval tower — breaking the sameness, beckoning him to ride there before he turned back to camp.

Taking a look around him, as he had at intervals, he stopped short. Four riders followed him steadily. Four white men not visible minutes ago, else overlooked during his intentness on the northwest.

He looked another moment and rode on, guessing the trailers to be Trumbo's idea, somehow.

Nothing changed as he held to the same line of travel. The riders maintained the same watchful distance, neither closing nor falling farther behind. Giving in to annoyance, he decided to make them work and spurred the gelding out of its ambling into a ground-covering running walk. Looking back, he saw them pick up the gait.

Not until Martin turned northwest toward the timbered creek and the peak did the riders switch tactics. They cut across, one running his horse in front and waving. Enough of the game, Martin decided and halted.

His pique heated up when he recognized the man Trumbo had called Coley, who yelled, "You're headed wrong! Indians out this way yesterday!"

Martin didn't answer him at once. "Didn't Trumbo send a crew out here this morning? I heard a Sharps until a while ago. No Indians' rifles."

"Enough men in that outfit to take care themselves," Coley said. He used a measured way of speaking, of placing a thought in front of each utterance. On horseback he loomed taller and wider, a raw-boned man, thick-handed, formed of big bones and dark skin. The full, black beard fooled the eye into taking him for an older, stolid man, like a plodding sodbuster, until you noted the quick, black vigilance; then that impression peeled away, leaving the hard, taciturn, competent man underneath.

"Sid said to see you kept your hair," Coley continued.

"Well —"

"Ain't you his pardner?"

"Did he say so?"

"He did."

"How far does this nurse-tending go?"

Coley's broad mouth spread; for him it represented a grin, and he wasn't a humorous man, exposing spaced, yellow teeth. "All I know is he said keep you in sight — out of trouble." He reined his horse about, a movement as direct as a command.

Martin stayed where he was. Coley reined back, a doggedness coming over him, and Martin pointed and asked, "How far to that peak yonder?"

"Farther'n you think."

"Four-five miles? Maybe six?"

"Closer to ten."

"Too far," Martin differed. "I used to hunt with Sid."

"I hear you're pretty good at fightin', too."

"Sid told you that?"

"Uh-huh. I'm pretty good myself. I'd like to try you sometime."

"There's nothing to stop you."

"You're Sid's pardner."

"Don't let that hold you back, Coley."

Coley showed no fear; in fact, Martin

doubted that Coley would fear any man. Whatever he performed for Sid, he was no mere handyman around camp. He was Sid's main lieutenant.

"We'd better git back to camp," Coley said, revealing a rare uncertainty.

Martin didn't delay this time. That would be pointless now. For he had ridden alone into strange country, a reckless ride because of the always present threat of Indians. In truth, he'd meant no special reference to the peak, other than to demonstrate his independence and to clear up any notion Coley might have that he was a tenderfoot.

Before turning his horse, however, Martin stamped the country off northwest in his mind, like a map, acting from old habit. The flat-topped, tower-like peak rising to his right above the humping swells of the prairie sea; the creek twisting this side of it. Hunters went by such landmarks. A certain peak or butte or notch in a line of hills. Some had names and some didn't. Places where you camped if there was water. Signposts pointing a man to cherry-red campfires and friendly voices before the plains darkness closed in.

"Fair enough," Martin agreed, not loath to turn his back on littered, cheerless country.

In the course of riding south, a tenseness

took stand in Martin and redoubled as the other riders formed around him, though not crowding him: that he was virtually their prisoner.

Just before dark Martin heard a wagon bumping and lumbering over the prairie, and saw a six-man outfit approaching the ford from the northwest. He watched three double teams of mules lurch as they entered the shallow stream, straining in the sandy mud, kicking up water, while riders on both sides of the laden hide wagon spurred mounts to pull harder on ropes tied to the frame.

The short cavalcade climbed the cut and paused, the teams heaving, while the riders freed the ropes and coiled them, after which the mules, sensing their evening feed, jangled straightway for camp. What continued to hold Martin's attention was the wagon itself, the hides high on the broad rack, lapped and boomed down like a load of hay. Somebody had found a big bunch today, miles beyond hearing of the camp.

He expected the crew to pick an open place and spread out the hides for pegging, flesh sides up. Instead, to his puzzlement, the outfit made for the hide yard on the other side of the camp. There the driver drew alongside a long stack, higher than a man's head, and the riders joined in unloading the green hides upon the old.

He tried to keep count as the hides were jerked off and piled. Distance, plus the early evening gloom and the figures scrambling over the wagon and the stack-pile obscured his vision. At that, his tally exceeded a hundred when the unloading was finished, an unusual kill under present conditions.

None of this made sense, he knew, unless the crew was dodging the pegging chore. But an unpegged hide warped and curled, leaving a rough, uneven robe. Every hunter was aware that proper skinning and care of hides brought premium prices. In the old days Trumbo was a stickler.

Late darkness veiled the valley as Martin left camp, drawn toward the hide yard by the inconsistency that wouldn't let him rest.

All sounds in Trumbo's camp had dwindled an hour past, and the only sign of activity was Trumbo's light, burning like a restless yellow eye in his sumptuous house on wheels.

Martin remembered the particular embankment of hides because it was the highest and the longest. It extended now in front of him like a black hedge athwart the faint moonwash.

Reaching the nauseous hump, he moved

along it to where he judged the crew had unloaded and methodically, began feeling and pressing the top hides; pausing once — a long pause, doubting the rigidity under his hands, and working on and examining others, faster, roughly. He left off again, increasingly puzzled. To make certain he searched past the farthest possible place where the green hides could be. To make more certain, he explored back toward his starting point, digging beneath the topmost layers and several yards past for good measure.

It was the same. He drew still, hands pressing the crusty edge of a hide, deep in thought over an unmistakable fact.

These robes weren't green, ripped off animals shot today or yesterday. They were dry and stiff, as hard as boards — old flint hides, taken some time ago. He knew, and he struck the hide with his balled fist and turned, walking heavily.

Trumbo, an early riser in the old days, reached camp around nine o'clock, mounted on the buckskin. Coley trailed him in a light wagon. The skin under Trumbo's eyes hung in puffy pouches. Nonetheless, he was clean shaven and already imparting the excitement of the hunt.

Martin regretted now agreeing to go, but

it was too late to back out.

Trumbo yelled a greeting, dismounted and took a Sharps from its long saddle case and handed it to Martin. "Take a squint at that, man."

It was a beautiful killing weapon, a Big Fifty, the stock and forearm of polished walnut, and a telescope sight mounted on the long, blue barrel.

"Heavier than my Sharps .40-90," Martin said, nodding approval.

Suddenly an ease grew between them, and all Trumbo needed, a remark leading into a discussion of guns. The set triggers, he said — one used to set it and the other serving as a hair trigger — were so delicate he could fire the rifle by the slightest touch. And, he exclaimed, that was a full-length 20-power 'scope, a Vollmer, no less, imported from Jena, Germany; the plain cross hairs bolstered with upper and lower stadia hairs, fixed to cover a thirty-inch patch at 200 yards or beyond . . . Furthermore, Trumbo enthused, this particular Sharps had another surprise. It was chambered for a monstrous shell carrying 170 grains of powder, compared to the 90 in Martin's weapon, and a slug of 700 grains of lead.

Martin stared. "Christ, Sid — this thing is a cannon."

"Why use two bullets? It's a dirty, stinking trade. Better get it the quickest way you can."

"Rate of kill must be fast enough," Martin said. "I've yet to see a live buffalo in Texas."

"Don't worry — you'll see 'em today — plenty," Trumbo promised. In contradiction, he appeared in no hurry to depart and swung back to guns, explaining the improvements in the Sharps since Martin had hunted. He said he also owned an "Old Reliable" Sharps, a .45-120-550, of which only two thousand were made. A marvelous weapon weighing sixteen pounds. It was in the wagon and Martin was welcome to use it today.

"I'll stick to the old .40-90. I'm used to it — or was."

Trumbo talked on. In between he drank a cup of Augustin's pitch-black coffee and revived an old argument of the buffalo range, the merits of the Sharps vs. the Remington, stating his preference for the former's lever action over the ear on top of the breech lock on the latter, and the straight cartridge of the Sharps over the Remington's bottlenecked shell.

Thinking of the lengthy ride ahead of them, Martin glanced at the climbing sun and back at Trumbo. He reminded you of a man putting off, who'd rather talk about a chore than do it; and Martin's earlier insight rose again: Trumbo hadn't hunted in a long time. He was soft.

Next, Trumbo elaborated on the uses of antelope buckskin. Stretched thin, he said, it did as well as paper for patching bullets. Yes, Martin remembered. The endless talking bored him. His eyes wandered, attracted to the movement of a horseman poking along the Double Mountain Fork. Trumbo, — not noticing, was making observations on reloading shells. When Martin looked a second time, the rider was coming straight for camp.

It was the horse that produced the first start of recognition. A scrawny, nimble bay, mustang in size, carrying a slumped figure. Surprised, then angry, Martin watched Rip Burke approach. Burke took a tentative look of the camp, braced himself and rode in, his voice as gruff and independent as ever:

"No mail for you in Rath. Even waited around an extra day. Wasn't a thing."

"Mail — ?" Martin said. Instinct, not reason, prompted him to ask no more.

Burke looked more woeful than that morning in the alley behind the Palace of Beautiful Sin. The brim of his hat hung askew, indicating he had slept with it on. His silvery hair fell in ropy snarls, his oxbow mustache drooped, more mournful than usual, and his eyes were reddish slits behind low-shuttered lids. However, the stock of the Ballard rode cased under his right leg; and probably early during his bender the thought of dressing up had moved him, for he wore a new blue shirt, already the worse for wear.

Thus broke, his spree over, and suffering, he was back to ask for his job. Martin could summon scant sympathy for him.

"You're just in time," Martin said. "We're going on a hunt." A dingy pain clutched the whisky-gray mask. Martin turned to Trumbo, "This is —"

"I know Burke," Trumbo said, chopped off. "We don't need him today."

"We can use another skinner if we have much luck," Martin said, obeying an impulse. Did he want to punish Burke or did he want him along for other reasons?

Trumbo shrugged and returned the Sharps to its case and climbed heavily to the saddle. Martin mounted and the four took the road leading to the crossing. Burke hung to the rear, affixing hungry eyes on the pot of beans simmering over Augustin's fire.

Relenting, Martin said to him, "Eat your breakfast, then catch up fast." When Burke caught up in less than half an hour, Martin dropped back. "Why'd you show up?"

"Foolishest thing I ever did," the hunter groaned, evading. "Here you put a man to work the second he rides in. When he's still poorly from the grub o' that blacksmith that runs the restaurant in Rath." He groaned anew and held his stomach and a beseechingness entered his face.

Martin was unsparing. "Before or after your spree? I know why you're back. Hell, you're broke — dead broke. You want a place by the fire next winter."

"Broke, am I?" Indignantly, Burke dug into his britches and displayed a little wad of greenbacks. " 'Nough there to whoop it, if I was a mind to. You betcha." He cocked his head, and Martin saw the slyness like a bright bead in each bleary eye. "Maybe I'se afraid you'd git lost way out here . . . Roebuck, I know you didn't send me in for the mail. I had to say somethin' with Trumbo there. But I got a message for you just the same."

"Message?"

Burke's mercurial face waxed secretive. "From that Miss Sanford. She's in Rath at the hotel. Said to tell you she found a way out after all."

"A way — how?"

Burke's countenance switched to a cat's

grin. "With some soldier boys, sent out from Fort Griffin to look for her pappy."

"She made a point of that, I guess?"

"That's the idee I got."

"Tell me something else. Did Comanches raid Trumbo's camp last spring on the Salt Fork — kill two skinners and the cook?"

"That was the story in Rath."

A load seemed to lift off Martin's shoulders.

"Don't know what happened to the hides — if the Comanch' had time to burn everything," Burke said and, in a tone of duty well done, "Does that hire me back?"

"We'll see," Martin said.

Trumbo led them north, along the same general way Martin had taken the day before. He heard no shooting today. A profound silence gripped the rolling country, and not a single wild animal broke the monotony of the empty distances.

A moodiness replaced Trumbo's earlier high spirits. He took a bottle from his saddlebag and offered it to Martin, who had a drink. Trumbo drank and offered again to Martin, who declined.

"I know what you're thinking," Trumbo said, after another swallow. "We used to have a rule, didn't we? No hard drinking before sundown."

"Still a good rule. We got more buff and we didn't shoot each other."

"Times have changed, Martin. So have we. Remember reading in a book that the only thing constant is change itself . . . Never forgot that. Not that it helps a man; but it's true. You have to face up. I'll take the way it used to be."

"All of it?"

"All of it," Trumbo said.

Martin could understand. He missed the old times as well. Maybe that was the difference between him and Sid. Sid couldn't face up. A lot of hunters couldn't.

"There's still bone-picking," Martin said, jesting, and saw Trumbo's spurning expression. Picking up bones wasn't Sid's style. He was meant to fly high or fall far. No middle ground for him. The puzzle of the flint hides kept bothering Martin, but a deeper sense told him now wasn't the time to bring it up.

Short of noon the creek line and the falt-topped butte appeared in the northwest. Farther on, more west than north, miles away, massed the landmark of Double Mountain, remote and watchful above the rolling green plain, looming mysteriously in the glittering light. About here, Martin remembered, Coley and the others had caught him.

Therefore, when Trumbo turned northeast, Martin gave him a blank look. "I thought all the hunting was northwest?"

"Has been — was," Trumbo agreed. "Pretty well shot out by now, and what's left is scary and wild as hell. The boys spotted a little dab off this way yesterday." He pointed northeast. "They can't be too far." He flashed his smile. "Gonna have to hump it, man, if we bring home meat this evening."

He set a faster pace after that, pausing only to sweep the emptiness with field glasses. Twice he took short pulls from the bottle. Burke stayed between the hunters and the wagon, preferring to suffer the aftermath of his spree alone.

The harsh eye of the early afternoon sun was upon them by this time. Trumbo looked through his glasses again. Martin heard a remembered excitement quickening his voice. "Look — off there!" Trumbo jabbed a forefinger and handed the glasses to Martin.

As Martin looked, the slaughter's dreadful white litter stretched brokenly as far as he could see, in fields and meadows of bones, no different from both sides of the valley of the Double Mountain Fork. Slowly, he brought the binoculars from left to right and sighted nothing; then, shortening the range, he discovered motion. A dark object. It was moving. Not much. Just one buffalo bull plodding down a draw, prophetic in his enforced solitude.

"I see one," Martin said. "Just one."

"That's enough — let's go get him!" cried Trumbo, who wouldn't have bothered four years ago. Trumbo stood high in his stirrups, signaled the wagon and shot away on a looping interception. Martin jumped his horse out.

The afternoon was sultry hot and the breeze only a stir when they got down and tied their horses to mesquite bushes, took the Sharps rifles and rest sticks and began the approach. Their actions recalled for Martin that in the past they would have ridden within three hundred yards, ordered their trained horses to lie down, set up sticks and knocked down the leader to start the shaggies milling and hooking. Instead, in order to kill one spooky bull, they hoofed some two hundred yards to the base of the low rise overlooking the draw and crawled on all fours to the crest, bathed in sweat, hacking for wind.

When Martin looked, he was surprised to see how close they were to their game. A ferocious-looking bull, in his prime, his horns developed to a full semicircular curve, and he was obviously headed for water on the Double Mountain Fork as he lumbered south down the draw, following a winding trail, his black chin-mop almost sweeping the ground.

He stood six feet at the powerful shoulders, weighed no less than two thousand pounds and was shedding his seal-brown coat in ragged patches. Martin continued to observe the dark beast. How small and out of proportion the hind legs looked to the massive head and forequarters. How staring and expressionless his eyes. How stubborn he looked in that peculiar up-and-down motion, a plodding, tragic stubbornness that made him so vulnerable. Martin watched in fascination.

"Hurry up!"

At Trumbo's low voice Martin realized he was just looking. He set up the *bois d'arc* rest sticks, eared back the hammer and laid the barrel of the Sharps in the notch. He heard the click of the hammer on Trumbo's rifle and saw him kneeling a couple of yards to his right, down the rise and therefore slightly behind Martin.

Martin experienced little excitement as the huge beast loomed on the worn trail, coming at a nodding gait, the great forehead bobbing, the small black eyes unsuspecting. Like shooting stock in a pen, he thought. Everything was right. The slight wind nearly straight to the hunters.

And all at once Martin ducked down and he heard his own hoarse whisper, "Sid — you take him."

He saw Trumbo jerk, heard his startled, "What the hell!" as he knelt lower and sighted along the barrel.

Martin faced around, seeing the bull lumbering within fifty yards, cloven black hoofs kicking up tiny spurts of brown dust. Martin crouched lower in the grass and weeds, tensed for the blast of Sid Trumbo's Sharps.

Nothing happened. Martin dared not move because beyond where he was the winding path slanted in toward the hunters before twisting again down the draw. A moment. Still, Trumbo didn't fire.

Martin could wait no longer, for the buffalo stood out not thirty yards away. Martin turned his head to see what was wrong, and for a drawn breath he stared into Trumbo's eyes, and he saw Trumbo's rifle in his hands instead of resting on the sticks, while the deliberate clop of the beast sounded heavily nearer.

Trumbo seemed to haul at himself to fire, his movements too hurried. His Sharps boomed. Black smoke puffed.

Martin looked front, astonished to find the buffalo still on its feet. It stood glowering in the trail, back bowed, pawing the earth and lowering its head and uttering deep, guttural blasts, its short, tufted tail held high. Trumbo had missed.

"Look out!" Martin shouted. "He's charging!"

He was bringing up the Sharps as he shouted, the rest sticks forgotten, and hearing the bull's terrifying whistle and seeing the high-shouldered hulk rushing with lowered head toward Trumbo, who got up to run.

Martin aimed just back of the shoulder blade for the lungs. At the roar the black mass staggered and slowed down, gave an awkward jump and stopped, puzzled, the doomed head sinking. Pale blood frothed out the black nostrils and mouth and the bearded head sank lower.

Martin levered the Sharps open and reloaded. The bull made several halting lurches. Before Martin need fire again it swayed and fell on its side, raising a little whiff of dust, and the great head rolled and became still.

Nothing seemed quite real to Martin — the hot glare of the sun, the bitter taste of black gunpowder smoke once more, the stricken beast kicking out the last of its life nearby, the shaggy head still strangely life-like.

Trumbo stood speechless, eyes on the bull. His face was pale. Martin thought of a man about to get sick.

"What happened?" Now Martin's hands were commencing to shake a bit. "You missed him point-blank."

"Too much whisky, I guess — or my rifle sight's off," Trumbo said. He avoided Martin's eyes and chose to examine his rifle as though for some flaw, except his cursory attention betrayed him; and for a man who held his liquor extremely well, he didn't look drunk at all.

"You shot too fast," Martin said. There was no other explanation. "You're rusty."

Trumbo looked at the bull, glassy-eyed in the hot sun. Wind ruffling the thick, black hair appeared to endow it yet with faint, stubborn life. Trumbo's voice enclosed a certain dawning irony:

"Know what, Martin? This makes us even."

"Even?" So they were back on reminders of old debts.

"Sure it does, man."

"If you want to put it that way," Martin said, speaking wearily. "Except for the money. You still owe the money, Sid."

He pulled up his rest sticks. His elation after shooting the charging bull was entirely lost. A strange melancholy rested over the hot, empty plain. Half a mile away Coley and Burke were coming to do the skinning.

Chapter 7

That evening, at Trumbo's invitation, Martin sat around the camp among the crew, eating hump meat, biscuits, and marrow-bone gravy. Chagrined over his failure on the hunt, Trumbo played the host to Martin and found humor in the near-fatal turn of events as he related the story of the bull and praised Martin's shot.

Coley looked up from his tin plate, his bony face unimpressed. "At that range who could miss?"

"It wasn't the range," Trumbo pointed out. "It was the quickness and accuracy. I got buck fever, I guess."

"You?" Coley laughed outright.

Trumbo's jocular mood evaporated. "It's all over here, men. In the morning we load up and pull for Rath."

Coley suspended his steady chewing while he held his disagreement on Trumbo. "Still some stragglers around."

"We saw one today, didn't we? Just one,

146

The only buff any of us spotted today anywhere." Trumbo was annoyed. "So we pull
out in the morning."

An order. An unexpected one for Martin
to hear after the outlook for days of delay. In
a sense, Sid was obliging him. Things were
about to turn his way at last, and soon he
could leave this shot-out dreariness.

Coley argued no more. Talk fell off
around the fire. The dusky glow of evening
was hard-dying, delaying the coming of
night, before the cool prairie was plunged
into purple darkness and the wind rose in
the southwest.

The stubborn light, the pungent smells,
the rough crew, the haze over the prairie
turned Martin's thoughts again to the lone
bull. He let his gaze wander toward the fork
and he noticed a figure — a man observing
the camp from nearby. Very straight, very
lean, a pack slung over one shoulder. He
eyed the crew distrustfully, but without visible fear.

Trumbo discovered him a moment later.
"Come in," he invited. "Have supper. Plenty
of meat."

"I will partake of your fire," the man replied, dipping his head in recognition of the
greeting. His walk was energetic and he
lashed critical stares at the piles of hides as he

came in. "I smelled your camp before I saw your light," he said and, taking an unobtrusive place to Martin's left, knelt to delve into his light pack. He drew out a boxlike, wooden coffee grinder, of all things, and a blackened pot and a sack of coffee beans. Briskly efficient, he ground some beans, poured water from his canteen and sat the pot on rocks by the low mesquite fire. That done, he pushed back his dinky little flat-topped hat and hunkered down to wait, drawing his neat brown coat about him.

Trumbo and the crew were all eyes, for the moment too dumbfounded to take offense at the visitor's brusqueness. Indeed, Martin could see, he was a baffling individual even for buffalo country, which attracted all sorts. A slim, wiry, clear-eyed man past middle age whose curly brown beard was turning gray, whose forehead and cheeks were as brown as an Indian's, whose evenly cut features bared an open censure of everything the camp represented. Even stranger, he carried no sign of a weapon, unless he had a pocket knife.

No more was said. The crew resumed wolfing supper, the outsider poured his coffee into a tin cup and sipped it, steaming hot, in between bites off strips of dried meat.

Later, as if the food had soothed him, he

said to Trumbo, "You will have to excuse my lack of response to your hospitality. I must be honest. You see, I deplore what you hunters — you hide-hunters — are doing. Rather, what you have already done."

"Guess you mean," Trumbo answered, his eyes showing a keener interest, "we've just about cleaned out the buffalo around here? I know that."

"Not only here, but all over Texas. There is a more precise term for it. It's extermination — of the entire southern herd. And if I may say so, it's not buffalo, it's bison. *Bison americanus.* True buffalo are found only in Asia and Africa."

He showed a nervous, intense manner of expressing himself and he gestured as he spoke, using his right forefinger to point and emphasize as a schoolmaster would use a rod while lecturing his students. An inkling began to spread in Martin's mind as he watched and listened.

"If we didn't wipe 'em out," Trumbo said, "somebody else would."

"True enough. It's inevitable. Also inexcusable. For example, when we see a great wrong being done, does that give us license to do the same? I ask you?"

Not Trumbo, but Coley took it up. "Buffalo's buffalo," he said, the sheen of his eyes emitting dislike. He pulled the long, bone-handled knife, took out the whetstone and ground the steel against it, meanwhile fixing on the other a stare as cold and sharp as the grating blade.

"Inaccurately so, yes," followed the non-plused reply, "and so shall the noble bison be remembered as a buffalo after he's gone."

He returned to finishing his meager supper, his air reflective and calm, and although he disapproved openly of the crew, his condemnation was somehow impersonal and resigned. Finished shortly, he brooded in silence, his head inclined in an attitude of discouragement. When he gazed about again, he regarded the rough hunters and skinners in a fresh light, a determination to chastise them on another point.

"Let me tell you what I have just seen," he began, and waited for the clatter of tinware to cease. "Rather, what I haven't seen. I've been as far east as Elm Creek, north of Fort Griffin . . . south to the Clear Fork, west of Fort Phantom Hill . . . north to the Staked Plains, from whence I just came." He pointed straight to the glaring Coley. "And what did I find sir? In all that boundless distance, afoot, looking carefully, I sighted fewer than fifty bison. Mostly old bulls. A few cows — and fewer motherless calves which no doubt were soon eaten by the numerous wolves."

"What about it, preacher man?" Coley demanded, longing to argue. He ground the blade faster.

"Gentlemen," said the stranger, and the formal salutation produced a ripple of grins all around except on Coley as the man rose with dignity, "you aren't aware of it, of course. But by slaughtering and wasting scores of thousands of dumb animals, you have committed a wrong destructive to nature itself and its precarious balance." He was, in his pent-up feelings, Martin saw, beginning to shake. His rod-like hand was trembling. ". . . Unless something is done right away — unless this frightful slaughter is ended — not a single bison will be left for future generations to see."

Coley lurched up. "You goddamned old preacher —"

Martin stood. "Let him alone. He's telling the truth, isn't he?"

Coley's knife glittered in his hand. Martin felt a flinch in his stomach as Coley stepped forward.

"That's enough, Coley." Trumbo's voice.

Coley stopped, not liking the order, and his cussedness seemed to go on as he drew himself up and blew out a long breath and hung a remembering look on Martin.

"You — old man," Trumbo ordered. "Make tracks out of here."

In silence, the visitor turned to obey. He picked up his pack, gave Trumbo a decorous nod and swung into his energetic walk. Trumbo rose to go to his quarters.

Martin did likewise, striding after the visitor. It was darker now and he could see the figure only dimly. He stepped faster as the connection fastened upon him; it beat stronger, with a demanding insistence, and he broke into a run, calling, "Sanford . . . Dr. Sanford."

The figure wheeled and started back, and when Martin got there, the well-modulated voice burst out its astonishment, "Young man! I *am* Dr. Fielding Sanford. How did you know?"

"Had to be," Martin said. "Your daughter is in Rath City at the hotel. Came out with some cavalry the government sent to look for you."

"So she's there and all right — thank you! I am grateful to you. I am late meeting her, as always. Time gets away from me in my work." Sanford's tone dulled, dropping into the now familiar vein of chastisement. "I'm not flattered by the government's so-called concern for me. Not when it's permitting,

152

even encouraging the extermination of the bison . . . Three years ago, you know, General Sheridan himself opposed a protective bill for the bison in Texas. . . . No — I have no connection with the government. I'm here solely through the good graces of several concerned eastern zoological societies. And, sir, may I ask who you are and why you know all this?"

After some words of explanation, Martin invited Sanford to stay in camp as a guest and be a passenger in the wagon tomorrow to Rath City.

Sanford's manner of inexhaustible energy dissolved at once. "Thank you. I accept, gratefully." He soon showed his fondness for animals by rubbing Tack's head, scratching him under the jaw and stroking his ruff and spoiling him with bites of biscuit from his pack.

"The bison is on the very brink of vanishing in Texas," Sanford sighed, accepting a second glass of brandy. "All we can do is try to save a few."

"By yourself?"

"That includes anyone who's interested in preservation of the species. You, perhaps?"

"If you can find the buffalo," Martin said, ignoring the inclusion.

"I haven't scouted northwest of Double Mountain yet."

"It's all been hunted hard out of Rath City."

"If any are left, I will find them," Sanford said, unswayed.

"Then what? You can't drive buffalo the way you do cattle. You might drift them just a little, but you can't herd them."

"So you've hunted bison?"

"A great deal — in Kansas," Martin said, thinking back. "I remember once we shot into a bunch. I wounded a bull. He took off and the rest stampeded. I got on my horse and followed. Pretty soon I noticed the youngest calves were getting tired and dropping behind. I rode in between them and the bunch." There was pleasure in the recollection, Martin found. "Guess what, Doctor? Several little calves followed my horse almost into camp."

Sanford, listening intently, tugged on his beard. "Why, yes, that could work!" His enthusiasm flagged as suddenly and he lifted a cautioning forefinger. "We'd have to put them on Texas cows, my friend . . . Or we might crate adult bison and ship them back East."

"You can't handle buffalo like that, Dr. Sanford."

"Why?"

154

"They'd smash any crate you could make. And how would you get them to the railroad at Fort Worth?"

"I see what you mean. If not, then, we could tie the calves and haul them in wagons to their foster mothers. I know ranchers who would help. Mr. Charles Goodnight, for one . . . However, that's not the problem now. Once I find a little bunch, I'll find a way to save some calves. I'd want at least six. You see, I came out here to make a survey for the societies; now my purpose has changed." Martin was reminded of Harriet Sanford speaking in much the same assured tone in Griffin. "I shall require some expert assistance, Mr. Roebuck. Someone like you who knows the bison."

"Not me. I'm getting out of all this. I saw the slaughter start in Kansas; ironically, I'm seeing the end here. I'm sick of it."

Burke wandered over, murmuring laconically, "We're bein' watched."

"Watched?"

"There's a lookout across the fork, one upstream."

"Of course," Martin said, feeling no particular surprise. "Rip — we've got a fast ride to make back here after we reach Rath."

Martin was mulling over the ride next morning at breakfast when Augustin, who of late had chosen to fetch all the old Comanche woman's meals to her tent, returned sooner than usual. Worry dragged through his voice:

"*Grand-mère,* she is not so good this morning. She no lak to eat."

"She was all right yesterday," Martin said.

"She is ver' weak. No eat. Not even the buffalo. Ver' bad sign."

Martin got to his feet. Sanford rose after him, saying, "I hope I'm not intruding. I'm very much interested in her as an aborigine. Your story last night indicates a most unusual type."

She lay on her side within the tent, her staring eyes filled with faraway images. As always, she looked small and weary to Martin. Very weary, he thought. Almost frail.

Undeniable sympathy caught Martin. He leaned in and saw recognition alter her set expression. The smoky eyes grew warm, favoring him, resting upon his face. The cracked lines in her face smoothed somewhat, and suddenly she smiled at him, a broken grimace.

Martin signed for her to eat her untouched breakfast. She responded by glancing briefly at the heaped plate, then away. He pushed it toward her, suggesting, smiling. Visibly against her will, she forced a trace of willingness. He leaned farther in and raised her to a sitting position, and felt the leaf-like frailty of her body. She slumped and swayed, but she did not fall. All the time her dark gaze followed him. He made the sign to eat.

At last, though uncaring, she picked up the spoon and took a bite. Martin crawled outside.

"She's mighty tired," he told Sanford. "The long ride out here was too much. We'll put her in the wagon before we start."

"A remarkable product of her race," Sanford approved. "I gather that she's considerably fond of you, Mr. Roebuck. She's eating to please you, not herself."

"Oh — no. I'm a white man. Augustin and I won't let her starve. She knows that. She needs more than food. She misses her people. I believe she'd go back to them if she could. She'd try again, even though they threw her away. It's a cruel way of life."

"No more than ours," Sanford said. "The Indian lives in harmony with nature. We flaunt it. We disturb its profound balance and cause waste and flood and drought, just as we upset the balance of human society and produce war."

Martin turned. "That was well said, Doctor."

Ten o'clock passed before all the hide

wagons were loaded and the caravan pulled for Rath City, some fifteen miles up the Double Mountain Fork. Trumbo and Coley took the lead. Next came Trumbo's house-wagon, followed by the creaking hide-carriers.

Martin flanked his outfit off from the dusty procession, traveling slowly in consideration for the Indian woman, who lay uncomplaining on the wagon bed. Sanford rode with Augustin.

Martin contemplated the hazy emptiness northwest, aware of his discontent again. The country there, in fact everywhere, was as silent as a graveyard. He could ride to the flat-topped peak and look around and catch up within hours. Except that wasn't possible at the moment. Not so long as Trumbo kept those two hunters ostensibly loafing at the rear.

Afternoon sunlight was slanting across the curly prairie when Martin saw the low outline of Rath City humping above the plain about a mile south of the fork, which some men called a river and some called a creek, depending on its high and low stages.

Rath's ugliness increased as he saw it closer at hand, brown buildings and sheds made of adobe and cedar pickets driven into the earth, the cracks chinked with yellow mud. And a large wagon yard, only partly filled, and a stout sod corral and a corner bastion for guards. Born in January 1877, Burke said, the trading post at its peak had furnished supplies, whisky and women for more than three hundred hunters and skinners until last year's decline. A sure sign of the times, Burke explained, was when all the women went back to Dodge City last fall.

Two years, Martin thought. *Just two years to kill out the entire southern herd.*

Today Rath City looked on its last legs as Martin rode along the short street. A scattering of bearded men loafed in front of GEORGE AKIN'S SALOON (the sign said), Rath's store, a restaurant, and picket hotel, on their faces the aimless stamp of enforced idleness and the vain wishing, he imagined, that the buffalo might yet return and times would be good again.

After Sanford left them at the hotel, Martin led on to look for a camping place. Meanwhile, Trumbo was circling his wagons in behind the yard, drawing the men on the street to watch the now-rare sight of hide wagons coming in.

Just beyond the settlement Martin saw two covered wagons and a house-wagon similar to Trumbo's parked between them. A man resting in the shade of the first wagon watched while Martin and his outfit passed. There was no sign of the cavalry detachment.

While Augustin and Burke were setting up the Indian woman's tent, Martin helped her down from the wagon. She thanked him with her smoky eyes and, attempting to walk alone, swayed and would have fallen had he not steadied her. He guided her to the tent, where she turned to him and made the sign for Horse and Here, whimsical requests to be sure. Yet he could do no less than humor her a little and so he brought the mare and picketed her closeby where the old woman might watch her graze. When he left, the Comanche was sitting cross-legged in her elfin doorway, her upturned features to the sinking sun, northwest, in longing.

A man was waiting for Martin when he returned to the wagon. He felt a perk of interest after a moment as he recognized Kyle, the long-haired hotel clerk on duty the night of Martin's visit with Ruby Hillyard. Dressed in the rough garb of the hunter, Kyle was in his proper element at last.

"Miss Ruby wants to see you," Kyle said.

Martin took in the house-wagon a hundred yards away. "So that's her wagon? I should have guessed it. What does she want?"

"Didn't say. But she wants to see you right away." Kyle, Martin gathered, was blending politeness with insistence and finding the mixture awkward.

"Tell her I'll be over pretty soon."

Later, walking across to the house-wagon, he went up the short steps and knocked, and the confident voice he remembered invited him inside. Closing the door behind him, he glanced about at the unexpected luxury, which surpassed even Trumbo's self-indulgent quarters. Everything looked red, a dark, rich red — the velvet drapes at the windows, the small velvet-covered sofa and the carved back, the upholstered chairs, the expensive carpeting splashed with gaudy yellow roses — and all at once he connected it: the wagon was furnished in the same taste and style as her apartment in the Hillyard House.

He didn't see her. In the next moment his eyes trailed to the movement of a door that was opening on another room, a reddish bedroom, and in the doorway he saw Ruby Hillyard. His eyes went first to the perfection of her olive-tinted face. She was dressed in a high-necked traveling suit of expensive gray; as before, her black hair was combed over her ears and knotted on the back of her handsome head.

161

"I told Kyle to tell you to come at once," she said, annoyed, coming forth and extending her hand in greeting, bringing to him the faintest scent of lilac. "Your face," she continued, before he could speak, "says you didn't expect to see me here. To tell the truth, I'm not sure why I'm here either."

She looked up at him and Martin saw her start to offer her lips, then hesitate. In that moment he read a swift appraisal of himself, but only for a moment, as she came against him and lifted her face to be kissed. He gave her a brief kiss and saw her expectation fade.

"A long trip," he said, "not to know why you came so far."

"There's always business."

"Business — what business besides picking up bones? Some hunters say the buffalo just moved farther north this year. Or the buffalo are late migrating. Men saying only what they hope. What they won't face up to . . . None of it's true. The southern herd didn't go north and never will again. It's dead — gunned down in its tracks."

"You speak with authority," she said, mocking him a little.

"I've seen one live buffalo between here and Fort Griffin. That's authority enough, isn't it? A bull I killed when I was out with Sid Trumbo."

"Prices are booming in Fort Worth," she said. "I'm paying ten dollars and selling to Eastern buyers for four times that, buying every robe I can lay my hands on. It's just a trickle, though," she admitted, "and it's getting slower every week."

He couldn't restrain his next remark: "You'll get rich on bones and cattle. You'll be the richest woman in all Texas. You'll have everything you want, Miss Ruby."

"Don't call me that!" she flared, eyes flashing. "I know my men do, but I don't like it."

"All right, Ruby," Martin said, and a curiousness softened his voice. "Why did you send for me?"

"Kyle saw you ride in. I wanted to see you. Do I need another reason?" She tilted her face just right, until he was looking fully into her eyes, seeing the force of her unquestioned will gathering, tempered with invitation. "Martin, I want to make you a business proposition. The best deal of a lifetime."

He was dubious. "What kind of deal?"

"To work for me. Yes!" She was hurrying him.

"I can't. If I could, I wouldn't believe you."

"Why? Why?"

"One thing, you don't need me."

She moved in, her body brushing him. "But I do — I need a man to handle men."

He could feel her fingers stroking his arm.

"That's it. I'm not your man, Ruby."

"Martin, listen to me! You don't know . . ." Her voice trailed off and her eyes turned toward the sound of a horse.

Voices erupted outside, growing louder. She stiffened in that direction and a tenseness ridged in her face. Voices ran together out there. Harsh voices. One demanding, the other objecting. Ruby stepped away from Martin, and he saw the outcrop of her temper, and the suggestion of fear, too, as she touched a hand to her throat.

She became rigid as boots scraped hard up the wooden steps, and her face paled when the door was yanked open and there Sid Trumbo stood, eyes blazing, mouth set. "Ruby — what the hell?" His flicking stare discovered Martin. Suddenly, Trumbo looked foolish.

"Just me," Martin said, dry of speech. "Ruby and I met in Griffin." In speaking, he guessed he understood her hurry.

She was struggling to regain her poise. "What do you mean busting in here, Sid?" But there wasn't much force behind her voice.

Trumbo ignored her to gape at Martin, who made his way to the door. "I was just leaving," he said.

164

Her could hear their raised voices as he walked on. His mind was opening and closing, alert to new meanings that disturbed him. But cutting through everything for the present was the hard ride to be made tonight.

Around two o'clock Martin aroused Burke, sleeping under the wagon, and in a few minutes they were riding north toward the fork, skirting the huddled settlement, a light in the saloon where Trumbo's noisy crew celebrated.

Martin did not confide in Burke. After an hour's riding, the hunter asked curiously, "What're we lookin' for, Roebuck? The southern herd?" and he let out a cackling derision.

"Not sure myself," Martin said, and related his discovery of the flint hides in Trumbo's camp, Coley's interception of him near the northwest hunting range and how Trumbo avoided that section the day of the hunt. Martin started to describe the flat-topped peak and the creek. Burke cut him off with impatience:

"I saw it — Comanche Peak, we always called it." His ridicule of a moment ago was forgotten, in its stead a solemn interest. "Last I heard tell the Causey boys camped

there on the crick. Fine fellows, too, Joe an'
Bert. A man was always welcome. We all
figured that was their range through there,
since they came in first. Nobody moved in
on 'em, 'less Trumbo did."

The sky was yet black when they rode
through Trumbo's abandoned camp, watered their horses at the fork and struck due
north. Martin let Burke point the way there-
after. Now and then the horses stepped on
scatterings of buffalo bones and the brittle
clatterings sounded overly loud in the night.

Once Burke said, "Tell you what, Roebuck. When we go back, I aim to find out
about that raid on the Salt Fork, when
Trumbo said the Comanch' came."

"Stay out of it, Rip. Rath City is Trumbo's
town."

Daylight pierced the eastern murk and
pink life sprang across the ravaged prairie.
Burke stopped and Martin saw before him
the dark trace of the creek and, forbid-
dingly the gloomy blur of the peak. The
stillness gnawed on Martin. He saw no life,
nothing.

Burke gazed up and down the course of
the winding creek, pondering the fast-
breaking waves of muddy light, and without
hesitating turned down the stream. A hundred yards on he crossed over and dis-

mounted under the thinly spaced mesquites and live oaks.

"Camp was about here," Burke said, looking troubled. Martin picked out the old signs: the marks on the trees, the worn path leading to the creek, the dim hoofprints. Looking, Martin had the cold sense that men had worked, scraped, pegged, mended, joked, cooked, and slept here not long ago.

Burke shook his head. He mounted and scouted off through the scattered timber. But a little way and he pointed, and Martin saw ahead the blackened skeleton of a burned wagon. The increasing light streaming through the trees exposed the debris, laying a ruddy glow on the twisted metal bows and charred ruins of the wagon box and wheels.

"Comanches," Burke said and got down to look. "Maybe."

"When?"

"Looks fresh. Few days — maybe a week."

Martin sniffed. "Smells fresh."

Both men started going over the ground afoot. For a camp where the Causey brothers had lived for months, Martin saw, the place was remarkably tidy. No heap of rusting cans, no whisky or liniment bottles. None of the trash hunters accumulated.

He looked for the wood pile and found scattered chips, no chopping log. He paced back and forth, widening his search. Every-thing was too neat had Indians attacked. Al-though a raiding party would take clothing and blankets, and skillets and pots maybe to make arrowheads, he found not one cook-ing or eating utensil.

Burke was prowling beyond the imme-diate camp. When he called, Martin walked out, leading his horse, and saw the blanched spaces where hides had been stacked, and the dappling of pegging holes in the packed earth. The Causeys had taken plenty of robes.

"One thing bothers me," Burke said. "War party bucks wouldn't take the hides. Couldn't haul 'em off, in the first place. No — they'd burn the whole shebang; ruin it for the next white man."

Martin nodded in agreement.

"Man in camp's always on the lookout for Indians. If a white man rides up, he's so danged lonesome for company he waves him in without a second look. Any gen-u-wine buff'lo runner would. So the white man rides in. You tell 'im to light and unsaddle. Pretty soon you pull out the jug an' the talk starts." His voice sobered and he looked around. "Good way, too, to git caught with your pants down."

"This doesn't tell us enough," Martin reasoned, gesturing about. "Maybe there was an Indian fight. The cook wagon was burned, but the Causey boys fought off the Indians and hauled out their hides later?"

Burke's reaction was a doubting look. "They didn't sell in Rath if they did. An' Rath's the closest place . . . I don't figure it that way, Roebuck." A crease ran across his forehead. "Ever see such a proper camp place? Neat as an old maid's parlor."

"Too neat."

Their eyes met in a sort of dread and they mounted to scout down the creek. Wagon tracks went off toward Rath City. Old tracks, Burke said, which didn't mean anything. The narrow tracks of a light wagon to boot. They used the next half hour riding back and forth on both sides of the creek and found no meaningful signs, after which they passed back through the campsite to search upstream.

While the sun mounted higher and the upper search looked fruitless, Martin doubted his wisdom in making the long ride from Rath. Still, he couldn't forget the flint hides. There was an answer and it had to be within a day's wagon-hauling or closer of Trumbo's camp. So he went up the creek with Burke and again they hunted back and forth on each side.

They ended up looking at the rocky shaft of Comanche Peak about two miles away.

"No white man goes there," Burke said, anticipating Martin's question. "No reason to. Nothin' there. No wood, no water. We've come this far, though. If you say so —"

They loped over the long stretch swelling upward toward the peak, ghastly buffalo skeletons leering at them from the bright green coverlet of the prairie, their horses' hoofs ticking on the bones and sending them clattering. There was hardly a break in the litter all the way across; the bones wearied the eye everywhere, in a hoary frost.

Near, Martin saw the shattered countenance of the peak and the loose rock piles at the base, bleak, barren, forbidding, a continuation of the lifelessness behind them. Wind moaned high up on the broken facing.

They considered the place briefly. By unspoken assent, for by this time each knew something of the other's thinking, they split to ride around it.

From across the creek the peak had appeared smaller, a slender battlement rising above the waves of grass. Riding carefully on, Martin saw to the contrary that it was broad and sturdy. He covered faster, in and away from the eroded rocky mass.

He wasn't expecting to come suddenly

upon the wagon tracks in the short grass, curving in roundabout from the west. Old tracks. Light wagon tracks like those headed south for Rath below the camp. Narrow wheel rims cutting deeply into the sandy loam of the shallow swale; otherwise he might have missed them.

Spurring out of the swale, he followed the trace as it curled faintly toward the peak. It dimmed. It faded out. He picked it up a rod onward, lost it once more.

He rushed on. A feeling began to creep up his back. An oblong depression lay before him. The grass wasn't grown over it, and the earth had a raw look.

He dreaded getting down, but he did and dug with his fingers. The yellowish-brown earth felt soft. Sickened, he forced himself up.

Burke came flogging around the peak, calling, "Wagon tracks on the other side —" and cut off his speech to gape at the ground, and then he swung down and stepped in close.

As yet, neither felt ready to do what was necessary. Martin took out his pocketknife, but didn't open the blade. Burke, likewise delaying, went scuffing around in the curly grass, head bent. His right boot struck something. He knelt and picked up several objects, and turned to Martin, showing a man's curved-stem pipe, a pencil stub and a cheap watch, its face broken.

"Somebody got in a hurry," Burke said, "or they didn't give a damn. Stuff scattered all over." He stooped and rummaged in the grass, and as Martin stepped across, Burke stood and handed him a small notebook, remarking that his eyes weren't what they used to be.

It was, Martin saw, a little black book, the cover weather-faded and blotched. Small enough to go inside a man's shirt pocket. A memorandum book such as hunters carried. He opened it and scanned the labored, penciled entries, swiftly to the last page.

"Bert Causey's name is in it," Martin said, and saw Burke grow still. "His memorandum book. Says they had about eight-hundred hides ready for market —"

Shock spread through Martin, an intolerable feeling. There was no great hurry now.

Chapter 8

Returning to camp that afternoon, Martin saw two persons conversing with Augustin. A woman and a man wearing a quaint, flat-topped hat — the Sanfords. He felt his first pleasure of the day.

"*Grand-mère,* she is worse," Augustin reported as Martin and Burke tied up to the wagon.

Fielding Sanford, in his quick walk, shook hands with both riders.

"They bring medicine," Augustin said. "Two times they come."

"So you fixed her up some white man's medicine?" Burke said right out, impressed.

"I'm not a medical doctor," Sanford explained. "Just a doctor of philosophy." His tone made the title sound unimportant.

Burke blinked fast. "Sure, Doc. You bet," he said, sounding even more impressed.

Harriet Sanford stood watching, hazel eyes politely cool under the round, flowered hat. Her high-collared blue dress, belted at the waist, clung tightly. Her expression softened as she said, "Father tried to give her some of his herb medicine, but she wouldn't take it. I don't blame her. It tastes terrible."

"But curative," Sanford said, shaking a finger at her. "Yet I agree with Martin. Her sickness goes deeper than food or medicine. She needs something for the spirit. All this devastation has had its effect on her, too. Seeing a way of life destroyed in only a few months." He was lecturing again and gesturing, submerged in the rapid swirl of his thinking. Another thought seized him. He said suddenly to Martin, "May I ask if you've changed your plans about going back?"

"No — as soon as I can," Martin said, thinking to himself that would be after he saw Trumbo. "I have business in St. Louis."

Sanford looked downcast. "I was hoping you'd join me. I tried to assemble a crew today in the saloon. Told them I was going out to look for botanical specimens. They all laughed. One shaggy fellow asked me if I'd ever been kicked by a mule. Another inspected my hat and ventured the remark that I'd had too much sun. I had to laugh, too . . . They can't see why anyone would go north of the Double Mountain Fork now except to gather bones, and there are plenty of bones around Rath City."

"Why didn't you tell them your real reason?" Harriet asked.

"Too ridiculous to them. They'd never go to save bison. But once I got them out there they might help, just for the frolic." His enthusiasm deserted him all at once. He pinned a thoughtful look on Martin and took Harriet's arm and said, "We'll drop by in the morning to inquire about the patient. Meanwhile, if there is anything we can do . . ."

"Shouldn't we come early?" she inquired, disregarding Martin. "In the event Mr. Roebuck has to leave immediately on important business back East?"

Sanford glanced from her to Martin and started his daughter toward town.

Martin flushed, then grinned at his own comeuppance. His eyes followed her. She held herself very straight, yet gracefully. She was different from any woman of his experience. And he knew now she would have traveled from Griffin to Rath in the wagon without complaint, and endured the stink of Trumbo's camp en route and thought nothing of either.

His mind was still on her when he walked out to the Indian woman's tent and looked in on her.

She was lying on her back, mouth parted and eyes almost closed. But she wasn't so ill that she was insensible to her surroundings, for she opened her eyes at once and in them he saw recognition and consideration for him. For a moment he thought of a child reaching out, and therefore he smiled at her. She seemed content when he turned back to the camp to eat a late meal with Burke.

From here he viewed the listless clutter of the settlement, like another frontier renegade of Griffin's stamp, but more prematurely aged, dying, in fact, after two furious years. Nothing had changed since yesterday. Ruby Hillyard's three wagons were still there, and Trumbo's hide wagons and Trumbo's mobile quarters. Did he sense a waiting? For what? There was nothing left to hold the town up.

As for himself, he had to wind things up with Trumbo — and he shrank from it. Not that he was physically afraid. It was an inward, deeper thing. By going over there, as he surely must, he would irrevocably cut his last tie with the Perfect Time in his life: a young man's first love and the trust of fierce friendship.

His reluctance became heavier as he felt the instinct to hold on, even while realizing he could not because it was already finished. Another time had come. A time to face up.

He took slack steps to the wagon, hesitated and put his revolver inside the wagon, mounted and rode for Trumbo's.

Oddly, it was Angie, not Trumbo, who occupied his mind now. Seeing Sid again had done that. He could see everything in vivid detail. Forgotten fragments. Something said, a particular expression or caress, and the shape of what might have been.

Trumbo's men slouched in the shade of the wagons, smoking and playing cards. One

176

was Coley, who trained his stolid enmity on Martin and returned to his card game.

Martin knocked and entered on Trumbo's hearty "Come in!" Trumbo sat at the desk, a bottle of whisky and glass by his right hand, a ledger book beside the bottle. Yet he looked clear of eye and steady of hand as he poured a drink which Martin declined.

"Where the hell you been?" Trumbo boomed, his eyes hawking over Martin. "I sent Coley over twice. You sure got that Frenchy trained. Claimed he didn't know a thing."

Martin seated himself where he could look directly at Trumbo. "He's a good man."

Trumbo's shoulders humped and fell, a gesture meant for indifference. He took a sheaf of greenbacks from a pigeonhole, rose and halfway to Martin tossed it on the lampstead by Martin's chair, much as he had pitched the sack of buffalo tongues the initial evening on the Double Mountain Fork.

"There's a thousand dollars," Trumbo said. "That'll grease any squeaky wheel for a while. I sold all my hides to Ruby Hillyard . . . Man, you fooled me big. You knew her all along and never let on." He winked, trying to jest, to imply hidden meanings, except the humorless inflection underlying his voice betrayed him.

"Funny," Martin said. "In Griffin she denied knowing you. I asked her. Why would she?"

"Ask her again," Trumbo shot back, striding to the desk. "Who knows what a woman thinks — any woman?" When he turned and saw that Martin hadn't picked up the money, any trace of friendliness was swept from his face. "What the hell? Don't you like the color of my money?"

Martin's mind spun faster. He had put off as long as possible. And so he said, "I took a long ride this morning, Sid."

"Ride? Where?" Trumbo sat bolt still. His heavy right hand, resting on the desk, slowly balled into a fist.

"Around Comanche Peak."

Trumbo opened his fist and spread his fingers wide and pressed them flat upon the desk. "You did?"

"We found the Causey brothers' wagon burned — camp cleaned out and the hides taken."

"Indians," Trumbo stated flatly.

"How would Indians haul off eight hundred hides?" Martin replied logically. "I guess it was an easy matter to send a man up there around the Causey boys' camp and fire a few shots every day for my benefit, wasn't it, Sid? You knew I was coming. Ruby warned you. I arrived at a bad time, didn't I?"

"It's your story," Trumbo said, not moving.

"You had to haul in late. You sent Coley dogging me that day. And what about other camps besides the Causeys'? What happened to them?"

Trumbo didn't speak. Martin felt the unchanging stare on his face.

"We didn't find the Causeys' bodies near camp. Been an Indian raid we would've. But we did find them in a shallow grave over by Comanche Peak. That's where we found them, Sid."

Trumbo's smooth-shaven face was impassive and he said nothing, a silence in which Martin grasped longer to the hope that he could be wrong. He waited for Trumbo to explain, to deny. Martin wanted him to. All Trumbo said was, "You're a fine friend, going behind my back."

"I'm not finished," Martin said. "I always knew you craved money, but I thought you'd draw the line at murder."

Challenge massed in Trumbo's face. "Prove it, by God! Prove it! My outfit's not the only one around here!" A dam seemed to burst inside him. A wild light glittered in his eyes. He lurched to his feet and his hands were shaking. His mouth curled:

"Listen to me — Martin, boy. You're lucky — goddamned lucky — to be alive. If you hadn't turned around that day —" His lower jaw hung. His right hand came up jerkily, as if to draw something back. Then he let his hand fall and clamped his lips together.

All Martin could do was stare back at him while the hunt reformed in his mind, gaining momentum, piece by piece, faster, still faster. The rise, the draw, the huge bull, the winding trail. When he was wondering why Trumbo didn't fire; and, in looking, why Trumbo's rifle wasn't on the rest sticks. Later, why Trumbo had missed a point-blank shot. A clarity awoke in Martin. He knew. Maybe he'd known earlier, in a way, but had held the truth in abeyance. He felt an actual sickness, and an actual physical pain struck him.

"I see now," he said, speaking just above a murmur. But his mind was never clearer. "If I hadn't turned . . . you'd have shot me in the back. That was the whole idea of the hunt, wasn't it?"

He was, it came to him, saying it for both of them. And all the great times lay uncovered before them, blighted, raw, ugly, false, no part ever really true.

Trumbo stood like a post, impassively. Martin, eyes cast down, turned to go, his mixed feelings beginning to straighten and harden.

"Wait," Trumbo drawled softly. "You might as well hear it all."

Martin turned back, stung by the malicious tone.

"I never could resist a good-looking woman," Trumbo began.

"You flatter yourself," Martin said. "You mean *any* woman."

"I said a good-looking woman."

Martin grew perfectly still. "If you're gonna say it, say it. Be ready to back it up."

"Angie," Trumbo said, seeming to pause with deliberate intent, "wasn't the perfect little angel you always thought she was."

"Say it, Sid. Exactly. No circling through the brush."

"I will." Trumbo twisted his mouth in a manner that enraged Martin, and he gave a suggestive jiggle to his head. "It worked like this, Martin, boy. When you'd be gone a while, she and I . . . well —"

Martin didn't remember starting across the room. He moved in a terrible swift haze. He smashed savagely into Trumbo and knocked him against the desk, aching to break him in two, to make him suffer. Glassware fell. There was no limit to Martin's strength or the punishment he could take.

Trumbo, a larger, heavier man, a powerful man, was punching Martin's chest and face. But Martin felt no pain. The blows on his body were as mere flailings. He battered the broad belly and the smooth face, feeling the heavy softness of the man, and somehow that feel infuriated Martin further. He found his hands fastened upon Trumbo's throat. He clutched and squeezed until the eyes bugged and the face turned dark red and the spongy body seemed about to wilt. An inner protest stopped Martin.

And instantly Trumbo broke free to lunge for the gun rack. Martin crashed into him. They knocked over the rack and sprawled clear of each other, Trumbo near the desk. He spun up clutching the whisky bottle. Deliberately, he struck the lower part of the bottle over the stove top. Glass shattered. The sour stink of cheap whisky reached Martin.

Trumbo came about, pointing the jagged muzzle of the broken bottle like a pistol. His face hardened, as inflexible as rock. He was going to kill Martin. Martin saw that will. Trumbo took two stalking steps. Martin moved backward, retreating toward the rear of the wagon, waiting for Trumbo's rush.

Someone kicked open the door and Martin saw Coley framed there, a six-gun in his hand. His black eyes groped for all the meanings here. "What you want us to do, Sid? Take him?"

"Stay out of this," Trumbo ordered. "He's my meat."

He closed the gap another step, and Martin spun a cane-bottomed chair in his path which Trumbo flung aside with one sweep of his left hand.

Of a sudden Trumbo rushed in crouching, forcing Martin to dodge. Trumbo pivoted after him. Martin, searching for something to lay his hands on, saw the coal oil lantern hanging by a nail. He snatched and threw it at Trumbo, who ducked and grinned as it crashed.

They squared off again, each in a circling crouch. And then Martin saw impatience engulf Trumbo, who could never wait. By these old signs Martin knew Trumbo was going to tear into him, headlong, almost before Trumbo did.

Martin was hemmed in. Dodging toward the stove, he stumbled over the upended gun rack. Trumbo charged at once and Martin, falling, glimpsed the jaws of the bottle as he hit the floor and kicked out with both feet. Trumbo held up. Martin's back jarred hard against the side of the stove. He heard the poker clattering to his right. He grabbed for it, missed, hand thumping the floor. Trumbo was coming on. Martin kicked again to slow Trumbo and reached and felt the cold iron in his hand. He swung the poker like a club, a short, chopping blow. It struck Trumbo's forearm. Martin heard the meaty whack just ahead of the crash of the bottle. Trumbo cried out and fell to his knees, cuddling his arm.

Martin was on his feet, ready to strike again, when Coley shouted at him to drop the poker.

Martin let it fall to the floor, knowing if he didn't that Coley would shoot him.

More of Trumbo's crew poured into the room. Coley, in disbelief at seeing Trumbo down, watched Trumbo for what to do next. Martin watched Trumbo, too. He wouldn't meet Martin's eyes. Instead, he glared at Coley.

"Get him out of here," Trumbo ordered, getting up.

Coley gazed at him in deepening surprise. "Let him go?"

"You heard me."

"After what he done to you?" Coley's black eyes were dismayed.

"I said get him out of here!" Trumbo roared.

Still unable to understand, Coley motioned Martin outside. Martin looked at Trumbo, who was turned away, and went out and down the steps, Coley right behind him.

"You and Sid ain't pardners any more," Coley said. "That lets the gate down."

During the evening a deadening inaction besieged Martin. He felt dull and without purpose. His entire body ached. Trumbo had battered him hard. Martin could leave tomorrow, yet he felt no particular relief knowing it. He could leave because he had seen Trumbo for the last time and that phase of his life was behind him. True, the money was lost unless he managed to catch Trumbo in court some day. Considerable money. But he couldn't take blood money. In its place he knew the rending truth or part of it. Except that about Angie. Trumbo had used that means of torturing him. Even though Martin doubted it, he would never know the real story. And likely that very uncertainty and suspicion, which Trumbo alone could answer, was Trumbo's wish to leave with him.

Martin reminded himself once more that he could pull out anytime. He would take the old Indian woman back to Fort Griffin and arrange with the army for transportation to the reservation in Indian Territory; that failing, leave her in charge of the post surgeon. He could. Except his mind shied away from tomorrow and going away, kept swinging back to the Sanfords and Fielding Sanford's preposterous scheme to save a few buffalo.

It was early when he left Augustin and Burke and went to bed in the wagon, to drop into a troubled sleep. At times he came awake, his mind churning in confusion, lashed by distorted images and mocking faces. He lay back, feeling the lumpy bruises pounding him again. He dozed again and fell into the drift of a flickering dream that took him back to Dodge City, and he heard laughter and he went into a room and found Trumbo and Angie together and . . .

He sat up suddenly, bathed in cold sweat, his body rigid, his breath short. No, he thought. No.

Before daylight he dressed and got out to stand by the wagon, reaching for the ease which had never escaped him at this quiet hour. This morning it eluded him except for Tack, who appeared dutifully, whining low for attention and licking his hand.

That morning the Indian woman became worse. She refused breakfast, whether Augustin or Martin offered it. By the time the Sanfords came, Martin knew he couldn't depart today.

Some of his depression left him when he saw them. They were, he discerned, so much alike. Rather exceptional people. Hopeful and trustful. Calm and pleasant. Gifted with insight and the courage of their convictions.

He received a mere cool nod from Harriet, who knew what to do without making a fuss. She was unobtrusive and efficient, without the self-assertive air of the militant do-gooder which he shrank from in women. To the tent she took soap and water, a washcloth and towel, meanwhile having told Augustin to prepare soup.

Afterward, when Martin and Sanford went to the tent, the Indian woman was holding a bright red handkerchief, a gift from Harriet. The old savage held it possessively; now and then she feasted her eyes upon it, but, Martin noticed, she didn't hold it against her, in fear he'd take it, as she had the comb and looking glass, which seemed long ago in Griffin.

She looked a whit better to Martin. The black eyes knew him and he could still see the flare of her stubborn vitality and her Comanche pride.

Harriet took him and her father aside.

The cheerfulness drained from her face. "She's failing fast. What can we do?"

"No more than you're doing," Martin said.

Her cool eyes said she disagreed and she looked at her father, who said, after some thought, "If you could persuade her to take a little whisky in warm water and sugar."

"There's whisky in the wagon," Martin said. "We've tried brandy. She won't take it."

Harriet Sanford turned her aloofness on Martin. "No more than she would the day you found her on the trail? The taste of brandy is completely foreign to an aborigine, Mr. Roebuck."

"So is plain old firewater. But I'm told Indians soon learn to like it."

"Your departure is being delayed by this," Sanford observed. Behind his eyes glowed the banked hopefulness of his new mission. But as if good manners barred renewing his plea to Martin, he held his silence.

"I can wait," Martin said.

"I almost believe you meant that," Harriet said, walking ahead of them to the wagon. Martin found the whisky for her and she made a toddy according to her father's exacting directions and took it to the tent.

When she returned, the cup was empty.

"She swallowed every drop," Harriet said. She set the cup on the camp table and turned around to them, a bewilderment rising to her face. "It's strange, the signs she makes. I had the feeling she was trying to tell me something."

Sanford lifted a hand to his curly beard, his alert being concentrating on her meaning, while his eyes shone in anticipation of some exciting bit of new knowledge.

"Maybe she's out of her head," Martin said. "The whisky?"

Harriet disagreed. "Not that. She was making the signs *before* I gave her the toddy. It's just now dawned on me."

"Then she was trying to show you where she hurts?"

"I tell you it's something else."

Martin watched her a moment longer, not sharing her concern or Sanford's excitement. To her any Indian sign would be shrouded in dark, cryptic meanings. Yet he said, "I'll get Burke."

The setting seemed more imagined than real to Martin as they arranged themselves around the opening of the tent and saw the savage old person lying on the blanket.

Otherwise, he could see that she had declined since leaving Trumbo's camp. More withered, so much skin and bones, a scant bundle of buckskin; the treasured red hand-kerchief clawed in one hand; the wizened face like parchment; the slit of her mouth more birdlike. Alive only in the depths of the black, beady eyes. There an intensity burned which he had not seen before, like a fever, and he thought of dying coals fanned to life.

His sympathy welled up. She was old and helpless, cast away by her superstitious people, by chance doomed to die among strangers, white strangers, instead of alone as she longed, and he could do nothing for her. No one could.

Even so, while he watched her and the unbroken silence prevailed, he had the unaccountable feeling of being summoned through some primitive cunning. Burke, too, looked impressed; if nothing more, his cynical eyes admitted respect. Sanford's brown face wore a look of delighted fascination as he sat entranced. Augustin crossed himself and steepled his hands, humility written on his honest face. Harriet waited in trustful patience, her lips softly turned.

Now Martin saw the veined right hand rise, saw the smoky eyes enliven and the sign form. An oddness rushed over him. The sign was meant for him. He remembered from before, on the trail. The familiar sign for male or son. A most simple and inmistakable meaning: the forefinger extended and upward, the other fingers and thumb closed. Meaning conception and organ of generation. An obvious sign.

He expected Harriet to affect the priggish modesty of her genteel background, to turn her face away. Pink tinted the white column of her throat, but her eyes did not waver.

The old woman's movements were not ungraceful. Her dark vigilance resting on Martin, she crossed her wrists above her heart, held them to her breast for a long moment; in offering, then, she extended her hands, still crossed, toward Martin.

His face became warm. The others were watching him.

Sighing, as though she must let the exhausted well of her body fill again, the old woman lay back and shuttered her eyes. No one moved. Everyone watched her. After a minute or two, Martin saw the black eyes open wide. She sat up and spoke a volley of rapid Comanche.

Martin got none of it. He looked to Burke for help and the hunter came to the tent and sat down by the entrance, trailing a wake of whisky fumes. She spoke again, a long speech for her, though it lasted but a short time.

Burke turned his head: "She says she's

very old. Like the Two Mountains across the crick . . . She don't like this place where we're camped. It's a bad place, she says, b'cause the white hunters are bad and the Buff'lo won't come back till the hunters leave."

Sanford leaned in. "Ask her where she thinks the bison went?"

Burke did. "She don't *think* — she *knows* — she's a medicine woman," he replied, a tone of arrogance in his voice. "The buff'lo went back into the ground, she says. Back to Grandmother Earth."

"Sorry to interrupt," Sanford said around in apology and turned back to her, absorbed.

Martin guessed talking about the buffalo gave her new strength. She sat straighter. Her black eyes snapped and her coppery complexion looked brighter and she began speaking at length. For so long that Burke interrupted her. Much of what she said was repetitious, as Burke related it. She was old and sick and her powers were failing. But being a Comanche she wasn't afraid to die. She had lived a long time. Her husband was a warrior of high standing when the Utes killed him near the Big Mountains. His name was Strike Bull. He was a war lance man, bound by honor not to retreat. He

192

counted many coups. But the Utes killed him . . . Her three sons, all dead now, were also brave and generous. How much better to be killed in battle, she said, than to grow old and die a natural death! And she told of losing her last son on a raid against the Tehannas five summers ago.

"It was a great honor for her son to be killed by the enemy," Burke said for her. "In his place now she has her white son. He is brave and generous like her Comanche sons. He bought her a good pony, a good tent, and good blankets. He gives her food. And the little brown white man" — Burke glanced at Augustin — "is a good man. Heap good." Augustin beamed through his astonishment.

"Make her come to the point," Martin urged, weary of her circling talk and her constant references of affection for him.

"On the other hand," Harriet Sanford said archly, "I think we ought to hear everything she has to say about Mr. Roebuck. I may yet change my opinion of him."

"Was comin' to that agin," Burke said, with a conspirator's grin. "Her first name for Roebuck was His-Heart-Is-Good. She's rubbed that out; she's made it stronger. His new name is His-Heart-Is-Big-and-Brave. Brave Heart for short."

"Get to the point," Martin insisted.

If Burke pressed her, she did not show it. She continued in the same roundabout, ceremonial vein, pausing only to rest now and then.

"She keeps sayin'," Burke went on, "this is a bad place. If we don't pull out, the hunters will kill us."

Martin asked, "What makes her think that?"

"Last night a white man rode around our camp. Circled it. She figured he aimed to steal our horses. Says he could've. She thinks he was after somethin'. She says we better be on guard tonight."

Martin thought: Trumbo or Coley? But why Trumbo? No law existed in this section of Texas. There was no authority to whom Martin could report finding the bodies of the Causey brothers. Furthermore, Martin couldn't prove anything. Trumbo was safe. So it wasn't Trumbo.

His attention flicked back to the old woman. She was weakening again and he could tell that her strength for the day was nearly spent. She rested on her side, the dull coals of her eyes first on Burke and then Martin as her high voice alternately faltered and picked up.

Unruffled to this point, basking in his role

as interpreter, Burke listened with a studied casualness, gorging his vanity. His face sobered presently. He pulled his hands to his hips and sat up. His posing vanished. He was slack-jawed as he faced Martin.

"Roebuck, she says her spirit will leave her body before long. Maybe a few days. The Breathmaker will come for her."

Harriet Sanford gave a sudden gasp. Burke continued:

"Roebuck, she wants you — her white son — to take her to see the Buff'lo 'fore she dies. That's all she wants. To see the buff'lo one more time."

Martin was speechless. Burke, he saw, was wholly serious. The Sanfords sat spellbound, in sympathy. "How can I," Martin said, thinking to indulge her whim for the moment, and spreading his hands, "when there's no buffalo?"

Burke turned, mixing signs with his bastard Comanche. Her gnarled hands described flowing pictures, pointing far away, to the northwest — vaguely, Martin thought — and made the sign for *Buffalo,* index fingers hooked like horns close to her head.

"She knows where there's buff'lo," Burke said.

"Tell her the southern herd's been wiped out."

"I told her. She says there's still heap buff'lo. A whole herd."

Martin chuckled. "You don't swallow that one, do you?"

Burke scratched his bristly chin. His eyes showed a sober searching. "She's got me thinkin'. Recollect when I told you she claimed to have powers? Well — I God! — she just told me she's a buff'lo woman!"

Martin's smile was humoring. "Sure. Sure. And where are these buffalo?" Long ago, he reflected, from the day he had found her, he should have seen that her mind wasn't right.

Burke probed again, using more signs than words, and Martin saw her repeat her gestures: *northwest. Far off.* And anew the meaning for *Buffalo.* Now the sign for *Much,* the clawed hands opening and closing rapidly.

Burke humped down in thoughtful silence. His beaten countenance bore a remembering, a wistful tracing back to old trails and landmarks under the open sky, to curly grasses and rainy-weather lakes and far-out camps. He seemed to shed time. He looked younger.

He watched her face, unaware of the others around him. He waggled his chin up and down once in affirmation, and again and again, as belief burst through upon his face, and when he spoke his voice imparted a lulling effect:

"It's a special place, she says. Comanch' call it the Medicine Place . . . or the Medicine Mound. Always plenty water an' good grass thereabouts. Always some game. Antelope, buff'lo — everything gits rollin' fat. Wild horses range through there, too. I've heard tell of it, but I never been there. It's a long ways."

Martin was ruthless. "Where, Rip? Where, now?"

"Up the Double Mountain Fork. 'Way up. Be three-four days' ride, anyhow, or five."

Martin's doubts rolled into his voice. "If game's so plentiful, how come you never hunted there?"

"No need to, in the old days, with a world o' meat just a whipstitch from camp." Burke grinned in his roguish style. "Besides, I understand Comanch' an' Kioways camp there a heap. Short-hair country for a white man."

"That's it, then," Martin swore, rising suddenly and looking around at the Sanfords. "She wants to see her people before she dies. Whether they —"

As quickly, Burke sprang up protesting. "She didn't say her people. Nothin' 'bout them. It's the buff'lo she wants to see once more. She knows —"

"May I speak?" Martin stifled his retort. So did Burke. It was Fielding Sanford's courteous, rational voice.

"I can see your reasoning, Martin. Yet there's possibly some foundation in what she has just related to Mr. Burke. She's very old and also very wise." Sanford's left hand was pulling on his beard. "Remember, she knows this country better than the hunters. It's possible she knows" — his right hand moved in a descriptive arc — "a secret place. A hidden valley. An idyllic savanna known only to the Comanche and Kiowa, thank God. In the breaks by chance. Logically, a place where the bison would migrate at precisely this time of year. And — mind you — where the bison would go by instinct, driven from their usual haunts. A familiar refuge. Nature's Elysium, so to speak."

"She's lost her mind," Martin said.

"At times that must seem so. However, her powers of observation remain keen. She noticed the prowler last night."

Martin felt ready to end the argument. They were all against him, Sanford influenced by maudlin sentiment for a scheming old savage, Burke because he was as primitive as she. Watching Sanford, he saw the naturalist's expression undergo a remarkable change, as though a light fell across his rapt features. Sanford stood and became motionless.

"I must be blind," he stumbled, and swept a look around. "I see it — it's right here before us. What we can do. We shall take her to this ah . . . Medicine Place, this mound. In turn, we shall save some bison."

"Bison," Martin said. "What bison?"

"A chance we must take. It won't come again. Meanwhile, breathe not a word to anyone." He looked straight at Martin. "You yourself gave me the answer. We can put the calves on Texas cows. As you said, we can't drive or handle grown animals." He stepped in, taking Martin's arm. "I hope I can count on your services. Mr. Burke will go, won't you, Burke?" he asked, turning to the hunter, and Burke nodded yes.

In spite of himself, Martin could not hold off the excitement that grabbed him. No man could stand unmoved before Sanford's earnest voice and smile, the persuasive force of his frank and unpretending nature, his bright and overwhelming enthusiasm.

"Will you go?" Sanford was pleading. "Come with us."

Martin's last doubts scattered. He was aware of the compelling and likable man facing him, of feeling himself swayed beyond his sound judgment. He was nodding agreement before he quite understood he was, and as he saw pleasure pulse in the even features, his mind went back to Sanford's materializing out of the prairie twilight at Trumbo's camp, like a conscience for every man there, and later to their long talk that night. That early, Martin sensed, he was caught up in Sanford's venture, unwarily chosen and imbued.

Sanford, in a burst of elation, clapped Martin on the shoulder and, in an excited voice that swept up Augustin and Burke, outlined his plans. He would purchase two good wagons, mule teams, much rope and supplies in Rath City. Day after tomorrow, before daylight, they would quietly break camp. Meantime, he would hire one driver.

"Be careful, Doc," Burke warned. "An Irish hide-buyer came in today from Fort Worth. Offered fifteen dollars for prime robes. Dollar for smoked tongues. If the boys in town find out any buff'lo's left, you'll see a stampede like a gold rush."

"How'd you know that?" Martin asked.

"Heard it when I rode in town this mornin' for my toddy."

"Better tell our Comanche friend what we're going to do."

As Burke finished, Martin saw the savage old eyes brighten like polished buttons. He suspected that mockery lurked there as well, and his doubts stirred again.

Harriet Sanford stood by his shoulder. She said, "You still don't trust her, do you?"

"I've agreed to go, haven't I?"

Chapter 9

Twilight lingered in mauve waves over the dark green floor of the prairie rolling and pushing against the horizon, revealing the distant humps of Double Mountain across the fork and the dim white blur of bone litter.

Martin picketed his saddle horse by the wagon and waited for night. It closed in with an abruptness in these high, rolling plains; it carried a little chill. Everything seemed empty and still out there, destitute of all life.

Rath City's few lights, greasy and faint, burned as candles drawing down to their stubs. It occurred to him that the settlement was dying by palpable lengths. Within a few weeks or days it would gasp and start sinking into the prairie sod as the lone saloonkeeper loaded up and pulled for Fort Worth, and the last hunter, convinced that the buffalo had truly vanished, cast about for somewhere to ride, where he might find a place by the fire before winter.

A horse clopped past in the early darkness. Burke headed for town. After his spree in Rath and return to camp, old Rip had behaved himself admirably. Tonight, no doubt, he felt another thirst coming on. Martin didn't call out to him. Burke had to go on his own, any man did. He was too old to change and he'd come back this morning. Let him whoop it up tonight. There was hard riding ahead.

Augustin knocked out his pipe and strolled off to his tent. Tack lay under the wagon. Later, much later, the great dog would slip away to frolic with his wild brothers, the prairie wolves; to return with the break of light, waiting in greeting when Martin got up to face the day.

Inside, Martin worked by lantern light on a list of needs for the long journey up the Double Mountain Fork. Having had time to consider the venture in full, he found it weighed less credible by the minute. Sanford's boundless enthusiasm had swayed him. Martin's experience protested the existence of another herd or a large band, even a small bunch; for he knew hunters. They rode good horses and they scouted country thoroughly before they devastated it and left it for new range. All the expedition had to go on was the dubious word of a cast-out savage whose worn mind wandered (a state to which Sanford had as much agreed) and who undoubtedly would scheme to die near her own people, although she could not live among them.

He put down the pencil, engrossed. If she proved to be right and buffalo ranged the so-called Medicine Place, then Comanches, finding game scarce elsewhere, might be there, too. On that unlikely assumption, he opened the ammunition box and took out his reloading outfit and a sack of empty shells and started to work, first using the crimper to make the mouths of the loose cases fit the bullets, next seating the new primers.

Reloading, usually done after a hot, stinking day on the range, was tedious and his hands were somewhat awkward after the long layoff. He worked steadily and his speed picked up as he placed the straight shells in the brass loading tube, poured in the measured ninety grains of black powder and tamped them without crushing and seated the paper-patched bullet and pressed the ball-seater down exactly.

It was late when Martin finished and lay

down. Burke hadn't returned. Martin closed his eyes, but sleep didn't come. Sid Trumbo formed before his mind as Martin used to know him: generous, strong, lean, reliable. It was a short-lived picture. Someone had said that the frontier brought out the best or the worst in a man. Some grew, some didn't. Martin slept then.

He sat upright in bed, awakened by a shot, aware that some hours had passed. To hear pistol shots during the night in Rath City wasn't unusual, except this one had sounded more distant and heavier, like a buffalo rifle. He glanced out the rear of the wagon. A fawn light was stealing over the prairie world. No other sound followed. Fully awake now, he dressed and pulled on his boots and quit the wagon, the shot almost forgotten.

Habit had its way. He stood still, watching the dull light streaking the eastern sky. He breathed the pungent sweep of grass smell. He stood motionless another interval, waiting for the morning ritual to become complete. He turned, expecting to catch sight of Tack slipping in from the direction of the fork, knowing that between camp and water Tack and the wolves had their playground.

Martin saw no motion. Never, never before, had Tack been this late. Puzzled, though not disturbed, Martin walked around the wagon and back, Augustin was stirring. He came toward the wagon, hitching at his trousers.

"Seen Tack?" Martin asked.

Augustin's face was puffy from sleep. He blinked in surprise and shrugged. While the Frenchman started a fire, Martin walked beyond camp. Daylight was breaking fast. He saw no movement toward the fork. By the time he had completed a wide circle to the wagon, he was asking himself questions. Would Tack turn wild? Martin couldn't believe that. Always Tack had come back. Always. Had a wolf pack ganged him? That, too, seemed unlikely.

They watered the mules and the saddle horses from the barrel on the wagon, took breakfast to the old Indian woman and sat down to eat. Neither man commented on Burke's or Tack's absence. But during the meal both hopefully scanned the prairie for the dog. They finished eating and Augustin, considering the ample leftover biscuits and gravy, shook his head. "Tack, he always lak big breakfast."

Martin saddled up and rode north. At the fork he turned left and scouted upstream for two miles or more before swinging back to cover farther out. He was, he discovered, not looking for bounding movement any more. He was looking for a shape down in the spring grass, positive that Tack was badly hurt.

He passed more scattered buffalo skeletons as clean as stone. He came to a level stretch free of bones. Just above the level of the short prairie grass, his eyes met a dark patch, a shape. A shaggy tan head and silver ruff. Tack. It was Tack.

He held back, unquestioning, yet unable for a moment to force himself to go forward. He rode across and stopped, recognition crashing deeper and wider. A mist got into his eyes. For a struggle all he could see was the stiff body of his dog, a soft breeze rustling the gray-flecked hair, almost as though Tack feigned sleep in the morning sun.

Sick at heart, Martin dismounted and took a closer look. A wild anger tore him as he saw the ugly hole behind Tack's shoulder, an extra large gunshot wound. Where a hunter would shoot a buffalo; behind the shoulder. He remembered the single shot, then; it had the heavy, unmistakable boom of a Sharps. And he saw, last, in greater anger, the knife embedded to the hilt in Tack's flank.

Martin jerked it out, wiped the long blade on the grass and scowled at it. A good ten inches long; bone-handled. Few men carried so wicked a weapon. Only one he knew. His mind seemed to lift a hand and point without hesitation. The thought kept swelling and leaping until it was whirling and shouting at him. A quick certainty flashed over him.

He stuck the knife in his belt and rode to the wagon for a shovel, dreading how he would break the news to Augustin.

Augustin turned still when Martin told him. Most carefully he set down the tin plate he was drying and folded the dishcloth and smoothed one edge. Suddenly the hurt protest gushed through his moist, black eyes and trembling mouth, and he looked down at the ground.

Martin went looking for the shovel. When he came back, Augustin was saddling a mule. Martin mounted and they rode across the prairie.

Upon their return, Martin hung Tack's collar inside on a wagon bow and made ready to go. His thinking became unequivocal as he loaded the single action six-shooter. The knife, planted after Tack was shot, couldn't have been a more plain sign for him to follow. He thought: *All right. Here I come, Coley.*

During his ride to Trumbo's camp, Martin

observed no outward change. Trumbo wasn't in sight. The morning was too young for him to be about. As usual, the crew was taking life easy. A card game was in progress. Some men were finishing late breakfasts. Others sat and smoked, waiting. Waiting for what, it came to Martin, after the country was gutted; nothing left but bone-picking? He was searching for Coley's rawboned shape. He didn't see Coley, and *that* was unusual.

An icy sensation ruffled up his back. He was beginning to understand now. They were waiting for him to ride up just a he was doing. He halted near the first wagon and saw the faces turn his way as one. Martin spoke:

"Where is he?"

"Who?"

"Now just who would I mean?"

The man pretended ignorance. He shrugged off a reply. Another man said, "If it's Coley, he just went to the store for some tobacco," and he nodded toward the wagon yard, which lay between the camp and the settlement.

Martin turned to look and understood when he saw the tangle of hide and freight wagons, some broken, and a long picket shed which served as a blacksmith shop. Today it was silent, its dingy maw empty; this, too, was unusual. Wherever Coley was in there, he had chosen a place advantageous to a man afoot, where a horseman couldn't turn quickly and was exposed.

All the bearded faces were upturned on Martin. He saw their covert anticipation. He rode to the edge of the wagon yard, dismounted and tied his horse to a wheel spoke. He drew the pistol and started walking, feeling Coley's long-bladed knife inside his belt. He wasn't quite sure why he'd brought it.

Ahead of him the yard and the town yawned in the warm drowse of morning. Small sounds from the street on the other side of the single line of buildings reached him, magnified in the stillness: a man's voice, the chop of a trotting horse. Someone was mumbling a song in the saloon. The indistinct words strayed away. A fat man waddled out the rear door of the restaurant, emptied a dishpan of water on the ground, looked at Martin and hurried back inside.

Martin neither hurried nor dallied. He held a steady walk, careful to keep the blacksmith shop in sight. Its openness bothered him, its murky interior and what he could not see. Therefore, he angled to his right so as to place something between him and the shop, watching the forest of wagon frames and under the running gears of the wagons. Coley wasn't this side of the blacksmith shed. If he planned an open fight, he would have come out by now.

Martin walked along the shed's picket wall to the rear. He drew in a breath, let it out, breathed deeply and stepped around the corner and a moment after felt his body relax. He repeated the maneuver at the other corner and came along the side toward the front of the shop, eying the few hide wagons between the smithy's and the town's buildings. Where was Coley?

A paced, ridiculing voice from within the shop flung him around: "I wondered when you'd come, Mr. Roebuck. I been waitin' right here."

"Come out," Martin said, "you dog-killing sonofabitch."

"Naw. You'll have to come in an' git me. You will — 'cause you're plumb riled up. I figured that, Mr. Roebuck."

"You're one smart sonofabitch, Coley. And yellow. All yellow."

Coley's bare laugh seemed to hang. "You can't git me in the open by callin' me bad names. Naw sir, Mr. Roebuck. Come on inside. I got me another big knife. Gonna slice you up for what you done to Sid."

So that was it. Martin's impatience soared. But there was only one entrance and he wasn't about to bull in there outlined against the light, unable to spot Coley in the dimness. He hunted up and down the flimsy wall for an opening. Once the cedar pickets had been chinked; some were beginning to sag. Martin seized a stake and tugged. The cedar bent. A sharp crackling sounded and he jumped backward before Coley's pistol blasted. Martin counted two shots.

He changed directions, quickening toward the front, and kicked at a loose picket. Coley fired twice again, wasteful of his bullets. He was shooting unusually fast. Martin, kneeling by the doorway, could see the blocky shape of the anvil mounted on a log chunk. He threw a random shot. Coley fired back, wildly. That was five shots, Martin thought, and it wasn't like Coley to panic.

Ducking low, Martin ran in behind the anvil without drawing a shot. His chest was pounding. He breathed the scorched smell of the place. He strained to locate Coley in the stinking grayish-black gloom back there. Light filtering in from cracks in the roof exposed the square bulge of the forge and the high frame of the top and braces of a light buggy, one front wheel off and the axle resting low on another piece of log.

Martin's eyes were adjusting to the dimness. He left the anvil at a crouch and took pounding steps to the forge.

"Keep comin'," Coley called. "I want you in close." His voice seemed to rise from behind the buggy. Martin fired once.

"That's your second shot," Coley called. "When you're empty, I'm comin' to slice you up."

As Coley finished, Martin heard a rattling noise. He fired quickly and Coley's grunting laugh followed when a gray cat darted forth. Martin fired again, a rod over to the right. But no outcry came and no taunt, either. No sound whatever.

Pressure squeezed against Martin. He caught a puzzling sound, like a strain or grunt. He turned with slow care to his left, hearing the buggy squeak and bestir itself an instant before he saw it rise darkly and keel over and crash. He froze in that direction, unprepared for the beat of boots rushing around the forge on his right.

Martin emptied his pistol at Coley and knew that he had missed. Coley was upon him before he could swing the weapon. He dropped it to grab for Coley's upraised arm flashing the long knife. He clutched with both hands and held, in turn taking blows from Coley's left fist. The man was horse-stout and determined. Martin gave ground.

Grunting, heaving, they struggled in a violent circle that swung them back and forth toward the doorway. They crashed into the picket wall and bounced off to smash against the hip-high anvil. Martin was too stunned to react for a moment and he could feel the same momentary inaction in Coley. On instinct, throwing all his strength together, he slammed Coley's right hand down across the face of the anvil. Coley cursed. It wasn't a disabling blow, but the knife dropped free.

Coley lunged for it. Martin slugged him away, reeling. Coley sprang up, no worse for the battering. He stood in the light of the shed's doorway, legs braced. Blood ran down his mouth. A greasy cocksureness enveloped his thick-boned face, an inflaming look that plunged Martin toward him. Then, not knowing why, Martin paused.

Coley continued to stand, to wait with a strange hesitation. His hands were empty.

Martin's left hand touched the knife at his belt. He drew it with his right and advanced a step. Coley flinched back. It was impulse alone that sent Martin jamming the blade under the base of the anvil and jerking upward. The blade snapped. Martin pitched the handle aside. He spread his hands, aching to get hold of Coley.

"All right," Martin said.

It was happening even before Martin

ceased speaking. Coley's expression didn't change. His right hand was sliding inside his pocket. Late, Martin dived forward, low. They collided and rolled over and over, struggling, Martin glimpsed, for a little handgun or derringer.

A muffled shot exploded underneath Martin. He waited for the pain to strike; none came. Coley's mouth opened. He went limp and Martin got up.

A large splotch was spreading over Coley's shirt. He was gasping. His black eyes mirrored an inward staring; they appeared to lose all interest in Martin and, after a few moments, all awareness of him. His fingers were still clutching the hideout gun.

Martin retrieved his own pistol and came back, looked again at Coley and went outside.

Faces like cautious owls peered from the rear doors of the store buildings. Martin reached his horse and mounted. Riding toward Trumbo's crew, he saw their grudging surprise and their respect, too, for violence was something they understood.

Sid Trumbo stood on the steps of his quarters, his yellow hair mussed, his face swollen. His manner communicated nothing.

"Coley's dead," Martin flung at him and rode on.

Midmorning passed slowly for Martin, in
an aftermath of unreality. Nevertheless, he
had shot a man and here the hour was only
nine-thirty. His feelings were mixed. Coley
had forced him to kill him, which Martin
had resolved to do but did not like now. But
he was going to miss Tack much, much
longer than he would regret Coley's death.
You never forgot a good dog. Already the
camp seemed forlorn, bereft of its most constant friend. Augustin went about his chores
with downcast eyes, and Martin forced himself to continue preparations for the journey
up the fork. Burke's absence was of no im-
portance just now.

Martin saw a covered freight wagon drawn
by six mules swing away from town. Two
men rode the seat. One was Sanford, who in-
troduced the driver as a man named Witt.
Sanford climbed down and took Martin
aside, voluble and excited. The wagon, he
said, was stout enough to haul the bison
calves, securely tied, of course, or possibly
they could be led behind the wagon.

"We'll see," Martin said and smiled a
little, "*after* we get them. As for leading a
buffalo . . ." He smiled again.

In addition, Sanford went on, his enthusiasm increasing with the telling, he had

purchased a lighter wagon for Harriet and himself and an extra saddle horse.

"She's going?"

Sanford's eyebrows arched up. "She can handle a team as well as most men. And she has patience. I wouldn't think of making her stay behind."

If Sanford knew of the gunfight, and no doubt he did, coming from town, his good manners forbade his mentioning it. He was soon flying around the camp, now asking Martin's suggestions, now giving an order to Witt, a slow-moving man.

"Got a gun?" Martin asked Sanford.

"Never owned one in my life."

"Get one. A good rifle. If we find buffalo, there's a strong chance we'll find Indians, too." They were out of earshot of Witt, who was conversing with Augustin. Martin studied him. Had he seen the man before? He grasped for the connection, if any; it hovered a moment in his mind and fluttered away. "What do you know about Witt?"

"Very little. I hired him in Rath's store. Said he'd been employed as a skinner with several hide outfits, worked as a teamster out of Fort Griffin." Sanford's enthusiasm rose again. "What sold me was that he didn't ask questions like the other men."

"Most men would," Martin said, considering Witt again. Was it at Griffin? Maybe he hadn't seen him.

Sanford's unlimited fervor, his ready willingness and obvious integrity of purpose, his earnest wish to do good, a real good — these qualities, Martin saw, were infectious, though impractical, and as natural for Sanford as selfishness and destruction were for most men.

Martin's letdown lifted a bit. He told Sanford about Tack and saw the naturalist's swift indignation and anger; and about Coley and saw Sanford's unspoken rebuke. Afterward, explaining his purchase of the mules, Sanford said he knew they would require grain and grain must be hauled; however, mules were faster than oxen or horses and speed was important. He estimated the mules would average twenty miles a day in rolling country. Because of the heat, the train should "noon" a while before moving on until late afternoon.

Martin agreed. Sanford had planned better than expected.

A rolling sound, a creaking and rattling, a jangling of harness chains and shouting drivers caused both men to turn. A line of wagons was snaking around from behind Rath City. Martin saw Trumbo's house-wagon and Trumbo on his nervous buckskin. All Trumbo's wagons were leaving, all running empty.

"Isn't that Trumbo?" A question beyond mere recognition hung in Sanford's voice.

"It is. There's nothing for him here."

"Wonder why he isn't hauling his hides to the railhead for more money?" An ironic bitterness swelled Sanford's erudite voice.

"Already sold to Ruby Hillyard."

"Admirable," Sanford said.

As the head of the train drew by the town, riders swung down the street and turned in among the wagons. More and more horsemen, until the train resembled a cavalcade. Past the settlement's few outbuildings, the wagons veered southeast to come in on the Fort Worth trail.

Sanford turned his head and Martin saw his comprehension of the exodus. "Rath City just kicked over and died," Martin agreed. "Everybody's pulling out."

Sanford's lean, youngish face waxed more bitter. "The end was months ago. They've deluded themselves by hanging on. What nature nurtured to abundance over the ages, man has destroyed in a grain of time." His voice fluted up in angry helplessness. He leveled a stressing forefinger on Martin. "Did you know that the bison is as smart as the plains wild horse, possibly smarter? . . .

That the bison is hardier than the longhorn?
. . . That it seldom has disease? That it out-
smarts the heel fly by cupping its feet under
it and lying down, while a fool cow throws a
wall-eyed fit and runs? . . . That it will fight
to the death to protect its young?" He
clipped off his speech on the brink of another utterance and let his hand fall.
"Sometimes I ask myself: What good does it
do to know all these things? Why did I come
here?"

Sanford's discouragement, rare indeed
for him, aroused Martin's sympathy. One
graying, middle-aged man, he thought,
lacking in great physical strength and a
stranger to violence, on a mission which a
betting man would give odds was certain to
fail. In which, Martin knew in himself, he
did not believe. But he said:

"Let's see what happens."

He expected to see signs of breaking camp
around Ruby Hillyard's three wagons, but
saw none and dismissed the move as too
early.

Sanford's enthusiasm had returned by the
time he and Witt left for town. Martin and
Augustin set to work about camp. On the
mules and the saddle horse they refitted
shoes and filed down hoofs. After a late meal,
they greased wagon wheels and mended har-

ness; finally, Martin sent the Frenchman into Rath in the wagon to fill the list of supplies and to look for Burke in the saloon.

The afternoon was slipping away. Martin dipped water into a pan and began washing up. Burke came to his mind. Despite his chronic crabbedness and fondness for the bottle, the old rouser was worth his pay. A good deal of his techiness was thrown out to cover up the human fears of a once lusty man growing old and fearful of the future, since the next swale of buffalo grass no longer provided a ready living.

Martin pulled a flannel shirt down over his head and idly noted the lack of activity around the Hillyard wagons. What with Trumbo gone and the game played out here, Ruby should be heading for Griffin. He was thinking that as he went out to the old Indian woman's tent. She was napping, lying on a blanket in the doorway where she could feel the sun. He backed silently away and turned for camp.

As yet there was no stir around the Hillyard wagons, and he asked himself why. Ruby was Trumbo's woman. Had been for some time. They did business together. Now Trumbo was gone. She was a wealthy woman to boot. Would Trumbo go without her when he could use her still, when he could leech off her still, when he led an exodus that had the earmarks of finality? Martin rolled that around in his head. He knew Trumbo as few men did, in his prime and these past days. An inner voice, wiser and older, spoke to Martin. Trumbo wouldn't quit a good thing. He wouldn't leave the country. Not unless Ruby was more woman than Martin thought.

Something didn't match, Martin decided. Responding to a vague sense of wrongness, he saddled up and rode across to Ruby Hillyard's wagon. There was no one outside.

The door opened before Martin reached it. Ruby Hope Hillyard stood in the doorway, her enormous dark eyes taking him in. She stepped back, an inviting motion, and Martin entered.

"I wondered how long it'd take you to get over here," she said, confident of herself. "I was about ready to send Kyle for you."

"I'm surprised you're still here since Sid pulled out."

"Sid doesn't run my life."

"At Griffin, though, you pretended you didn't know him. You sent a rider out, of course, to tell him I was coming." He was being harsh on her. The time for niceties was past.

"That was then," she said, her manner

dismissing. "Sid's gone. We're through. I told him so yesterday."

"Ruby, what're you and Sid up to? What's this sudden pull-out? If he went anywhere, it'd be back to headquarters at Griffin."

She glanced away. The rich coloring of her throat and face acquired a deeper tint. "He's going to Fort Worth to sell his wagons."

"You're still covering up for him. Still looking out for a man who would grind you up without regret."

Protest rose along her red lips, adding a heaviness, a discontent. Suddenly she said, "It was you I came out here for. I was afraid what might happen."

"It almost did on the hunt."

"On the hunt?" She looked unaffectedly startled.

"Sid was going to shoot me. Only things didn't work out."

"I didn't know," she said. Her expression baffled him. "I was just afraid."

"And Coley took his turn this morning."

She nodded in a knowing way. "I heard . . . I'm grateful he didn't make it. Martin, I really am." Her eyes were wide upon him, her face uplifted. "You don't believe that either, do you?"

"When you had my camp shot up? Had me waylaid outside the hotel in Griffin?"

She turned her head obliquely, her eyes not quite meeting his. "I could have had you killed."

"What stopped you — high principles? Like buying murdered hunters' hides? Like the last batch Sid brought in? By God, was that it?"

Unrest caught her face, a quickening, and in place of the hard-driving bargainer she was, he saw a vital-bodied woman and, he knew, a damned lonely one. She had a way of parrying a question while not seeming to, of almost making you forget you had asked it; or, if you did not, that it was unimportant, or perhaps could be put off and answered later, like a trivial game.

"Martin," she said softly, close to him. "I don't beat around the bush like most women. I know what I want, and I go after it . . . I like your style. Come into my life to stay. Anything I have is yours. I never go halfway . . . I can make you rich. Just don't wait too long."

Her face was different than he ever recalled, underladen in pain. She slid into his arms and lifted her head, bringing the faintest scent of lilac. Her lips parted a little; she closed her eyes. He kissed her, and became aware of the full surge of her being. After a moment, he pulled back. His hands were on her shoulders when he looked down at her.

"Ruby," he said, "let's talk straight." He held her more firmly. He saw her sag back. He saw an old look. She drew away, then, and he let go. "What's Sid up to?" he kept on.

Her face fell shadowed. Her vivid animation disappeared all at once, and he could not but feel touched. Her lips stirred heavily:

"He said he was going to make it big once more."

"In Fort Worth?"

"That's what he said."

"How?"

She turned to him again, in pleading desperation. "Martin . . . if I tell you . . . will you love me . . . just a little? Just a little?" Her fingers were caressing the front of his shirt. Her expression was open, filling up with the pain again.

"Ruby, talk straight."

She took no notice. "We could have a good life together," she went on, faster. "We could. I know we could. I'm not really bad, Martin. I didn't know Sid was doing all those things." Before he could look into her eyes, she pressed her face against him and held on to him, and he held her, too, hearing her sudden intake of breath and feeling her heavily and completely against him, un-heeding, while he sensed her loneliness and need.

"Ruby," he said, not ungently, "I'm just not your man." A long moment. Then he felt the pressure of her arms slacken, break, and abruptly she pushed him away. Her gaze whipped his face.

"You're such a fool," she derided him. Her large eyes, her heavy mouth, her vibrant voice, her slouched stance, the shaking of her head: all of her sought to belittle him. "Many's the time I've heard Sid laugh and say what a fool you are, what a soft touch you were for him. He never was your friend — never! He never intended to pay back your money — never! You were blind, Martin, just as you are now." She was, in contradiction, on the verge of tears.

His voice hardened. "You still haven't answered me. What's Sid up to? You still doing business with him?"

The explosion of her anger surprised him. She swung an open-handed blow for his face. Roughly he caught her hand and gripped it hard. That infuriated her even more.

"I won't tell you a thing," she said and jerked loose. "Get th' hell out!"

"Not till you tell me."

"No!"

She was backing away and shaking her head. Fury distended her face; it dulled her vividness and spoiled her looks. Martin took an instinctive step toward her. By then she was fumbling in a desk drawer. She whirled toward him and he saw a derringer blink in her hand, and her eyes looked wild.

"Put that down," he told her, his mouth crimping in disgust.

She hesitated. Little by little she lowered the derringer, and he said, "Tell me," as demanding as before.

To his crashing amazement she screamed for Kyle. Again and again and again she screamed Kyle's name.

Martin stepped to the door.

"Martin — don't go — please."

He jerked open the door to see Kyle rushing up. Martin didn't hurry. Kyle slowed. He sent a gawking scrutiny inside. He showed no great surprise. He made no move as Martin came down the steps and past him. Martin was in the saddle when he looked back.

Ruby Hillyard was clinging to the side of the doorway for support. She no longer had the derringer. Her face looked pale, her red mouth slackly open. A lock of her lustrous black hair lay across her forehead; she brushed it away. Her gaze conveyed bitterness, frozen in an image of accusation and unforgiving hurt. But as he saw that he also saw her features alter. Haltingly, she raised her right hand. It was an imploring gesture. He could see her desire to speak, to call out. But she did not, and then she drew back her hand.

A feeling brushed Martin; after a little, it passed. He whirled the gelding around.

The southwestern wind was rising, hurling the grainy grit like buckshot against the picket and adobe buildings. An empty tin can fled clanking and bouncing down the street, deserted save for one horse tied in front of the saloon, a horse that wasn't Burke's mustang bay, and Martin's wagon and team before Rath's store.

Augustin emerged shouldering a sack of flour. The Frenchman toiled to the wagon's rear, let the sack slide down to the tailgate and said, "Rip, he has vanished. *Pouff!*"

"Look in the saloon?"

"*Oui.* I 'ave look all over."

Martin glanced up and down the street, thinking that Rath City offered few places where a man could sleep off a drunk unnoticed. Burke had to be close to the saloon. Martin dismounted.

Two men were inside, the barkeep and a customer who looked like any one of a hundred aimless men between Fort Griffin and the Double Mountain Fork's bone yard, shaggy, unshaven, cheekbones a greasy brown, and waiting for something to happen.

"Where's Rip Burke?" Martin asked the man behind the makeshift bar.

The eyes below the shiny melon-shaped pate looked straight at him. "Burke? Rip Burke? Him? Why, he rode out with the bunch this morning."

"With Trumbo?"

"That's right."

Burke, Martin reasoned, might go to hell and back, but he would never ride with Sid Trumbo.

"So everybody's pulled out for good?" Martin remarked. The man nodded and Martin said, "Looks like you'd be boarding up? No business? Everyone gone?"

"Will, when I get around to it."

"Unless," Martin said, "they're coming back?" He got no reply and he said, "Mind if I look around?" and instantly he saw the old signs go up, the hunter shifting to face him head-on and the bartender hesitating before he denied, "I told you Burke rode out."

A voice lifted, a blurring voice, issuing from beyond the room, gabbling an un-meaning word or two. Martin froze and saw the others do the same. A dim voice, be-

coming clearer now, tuneless but recognizable:

"Oh . . . 'twas in the town of Jacksboro . . ."

Martin started toward a closed door
leading out of the saloon, and glanced back
over his shoulder to see the hunter charging
him. Martin turned and took a knee ram-
ming high on his thigh. The collision
numbed half his body. The hunter piled in
again. Martin threw a shoulder into him and
knocked him against the bar, which rocked
and chattered with glass. The bartender
steadied it and shouted for them to stop.

The hunter lowered his head and took
short, stomping steps, ready to ram again.
Martin punched him off. Ducking, the man
bear-hugged Martin and struggled to use
his knee. Martin tore clear and as the hunter
closed in, Martin brought up his knee and
felt it strike the groin. The man screamed
and doubled up on the floor, writhing and
clamping with both hands.

Martin ran for the closed door. The bartender, anticipating, got there ahead of him.
Martin grabbed his shoulder and crowded
him against the flimsy wall. He was short-
winded and flabby. He quit suddenly.

"All right, he's in there. Trumbo paid me

to keep him dead drunk."

Martin shook him savagely, until the eyes rolled. "Why?" Wattles on the fleshy chin quivered, but the man kept his mouth tight. Martin slammed him against the wall. "I'll beat it out of you! Why?"

"I don't know. I swear I don't. Trumbo said he'd be back — that's all. I was just tryin' to hold my trade . . . Burke's horse is in a shed north end of town."

Rip Burke lay sprawled in a litter of both empty and full whisky bottles. Plenty of whisky, Martin saw, with a mixture of disgust, as much as old Rip could ever crave in a dozen sprees.

Martin knelt over him. Burke was gabbling bits of the song. He reeked sourly of whisky and sweat and he didn't seem to know Martin. Spittle driveled out the corners of the whiskery-gray mouth.

Martin's anger left him as he saw only an old man who was pathetically sick, afraid, and helpless.

"Rip," he said. "It's Martin."

Burke groaned, trying to raise up. His rheumy eyes squinted open. A faint relief flickered over the weathered face, and then Burke sank back, groaning.

"Rip, I'm here to take you to camp. It's me — Martin."

The relieved smile strengthened. The eyes appeared to struggle toward something, a distant awareness, and the leathery lips trembled. "I know . . . heard you out there. Listen — I found out all 'bout Trumbo's raid on the Salt Fork. Little skirmish was all. Not a robe lost."

"Fine, Rip. Fine."

Martin started to lift him. Burke pulled back. Martin saw pain come into Burke's eyes, an inner pain. He shut his eyes against it, then opened them.

"Trumbo knows," Burke breathed.

"Knows what? Rip, talk to me."

The old eyes wavered, miserable and reluctant. "— 'bout the buff'lo," Burke said. "I got drunk. Spilled the beans." His voice broke. "Didn't aim to, Martin. Came to find out 'bout the raid."

"But Trumbo took the Fort Worth trail."

Burke clutched Martin's arm. "Sure — to throw you off. He's headed up the Double Mountain Fork, certain. Right now. Hurry." Burke was crying, the terrible, penitent, broken crying of an old man, and which to Martin sounded so much like a child asking forgiveness.

Martin hoisted him up and slung him like a sack of flour over his shoulder, and paused, thinking of later, and picked up two

231

of the full whisky bottles and went out, wondering how fast Sanford could get his outfit together.

Chapter 10

Later that afternoon Martin led the three wagons away from the dying huddle of Rath City and swung up the winding Double Mountain Fork, realizing little would be gained except a few miles and the practice of traveling and camping together. As they started, he found himself looking for Tack to bound ahead.

A contrite Burke lay on the wagon bed behind Augustin. Though stronger after cups of the Frenchman's black coffee and some light food, he was too feeble to sit upright. He couldn't be counted on for another day or two. Then, Martin knew, he would be sorely needed.

Sanford cheerfully drove the middle wagon, his newly purchased saddle mount trailing on a rope. Harriet rode beside her father. The old Indian woman rested behind them on a pallet of blankets. Witt brought up the rear in the heavy freight wagon. Martin frowned over what he soon saw.

Witt's vehicle was not only the slowest, and therefore would set the pace for the others, but Witt was no pumpkins with mules. The man was inept.

Near dark they camped by the stream, having covered but several miles at best. Not enough, Martin worried, when Trumbo had a head start.

Witt was slow at everything, from watering the mules and unharnessing to giving them grain; and when time came to picket the teams, he took them beyond the usual bounds of caution.

Martin went striding after him. Witt turned, his manner deliberate and vexing.

"Picket closer in," Martin ordered. "An Indian boy could run 'em off out here before we knew it." He was curt and he intended to be.

Witt shifted the picket ropes in his hands, a medium-sized man whose thick waist and thicker chest and blunt hands transferred the illusion of a bulkier, hard-bodied man. A surliness lay in the bearded face.

"I hired on to Mr. Sanford," Witt replied. "I'll answer to him."

That was the most Martin had heard Witt say. Witt's remark wasn't unexpected on the buffalo frontier where few orders were given or necessary, and go-to-hell independence was the rule rather than the exception. Instead, it was Witt's deep voice that dug into Martin's memory. From the first time Martin had seen Witt in camp this morning, something seemed familiar about him. Where? Griffin? Around Ruby Hillyard's store? Her hotel? Well, it didn't matter now.

"I know you did," Martin said, keeping a rein on his temper and thinking how desperately short-handed the outfit was. "But you'll picket back there." He waited.

Witt took his time. He toyed with the ropes some more, shuffled his boots; finally, still unhurried, he tugged on the lines and led the mules nearer the wagon.

At Augustin's call to supper, Witt was the first to fill his plate. Burke didn't come. Martin took a bottle of whisky from his saddle bag and looked inside the wagon. Burke lay flat on his back. In the fading light, his face was a formless wedge against the white of his hair.

"Supper time, Rip."

Burke groaned, drawing on the misery of his wretched body.

"Come on. Let's eat."

"I don't deserve any."

"Quit feeling sorry for yourself. Take a drink for medicine." Martin pulled the cork and handed the bottle to Burke, who, after a moment's hesitation, reached up an unsteady hand. He drank briefly, then at length, a gurgling drink, gagged and lay back, blowing through his mustache. Martin retrieved the bottle.

"Now you're going to eat," Martin informed him, "if I have to hogtie you and stuff it down you."

Shaking his head like a wrathy buffalo bull, the hunter reared up to a sitting position. "I God, nobody's gonna nursemaid Buffalo Burke!" he swore and crawled for the rear of the wagon, groaning as he did, complaining, "I'm no good, Martin. No good a-tall."

"Come on, Rip. You can make it."

Martin didn't help him. Burke eased his punished body to the ground, steadied himself against the tailgate, and wobbled toward the fire, every step self-willed. As though ashamed, he looked neither right nor left and ignored Sanford's pleasant greeting as he took a minimum of food. Chin sunk on his chest, Burke swayed back to the wagon with his plate.

"Rip's doing better," Martin winked at Sanford.

Guard duty shifts were decided after supper. Augustin would take the first watch, followed by Sanford, Witt, and Martin.

The cool, enveloping prairie evening seemed to fall faster about them than usual. That, Martin thought, came from camping close to town. Here you wanted the light to stay longer.

Returning from the fork with a bucket of drinking water, he saw Harriet Sanford walking toward him. She swung an empty bucket. He set his down and reached for hers without speaking.

She held it away. "You needn't bother."

"No bother."

"I'm quite able to."

Perhaps his earlier encounter with Witt and the certain knowledge of future vexations had strained Martin's patience; or perhaps he viewed her display of self-reliance as unnecessary and out of place. He took the handle of the bucket, feeling the firm warmth of her resisting fingers and catching the clean scent of her hair. Just when he expected her to snatch the bucket free, she let go and he turned from her, in silence, and walked down the grassy slope to water, let the bucket sink and fill and started back.

She was waiting a few rods away. The wind was cool on his back and he saw that she wore a shawl over her shoulders.

"You're a very stubborn man, Mr. Roebuck," she said in a composed voice.

"I grew up in a family where the men folks did the grubbing and toting. A bucket of water comes under toting."

"I see," she said, her air lofty. "A true gentleman."

He felt a remembering wince. Ruby Hillyard had called him that. He came to the point. "Your father's told you that I used to hunt buffalo —"

"*Bison,* Mr. Roebuck. Not buffalo."

"I know. I've been well instructed," and he finished: "— and did he tell you that sometimes I deal in hides?"

"All I can think of is the terrible, senseless waste," she said frankly.

"A true gentleman wouldn't do those terrible things, would he?"

He was mocking her. To his amusement she laughed and he sensed a beginning ease, albeit a constrained one, between them. They strolled on to where his bucket sat. He set hers down. She paused with him.

"I'm still wondering why you came with us," she said.

"I was invited by your father."

"I don't mean that."

"You mean why did I come when there's no profit in it for me? No tongues to dry? No hides to sell?" He spoke with sarcasm.

She withheld her reply, and he said,

237

"There comes a time when a man has to go see. If he doesn't, he'll always wonder why he didn't and he'll wish he had. If the buffalo is wiped out — and maybe that's already happened — your father would blame himself for not trying to save some . . . I happen to admire your father. I like him. He's a real man. So maybe I came because of him, and a little because of the old Indian woman — though God knows I'm no do-gooder — and maybe just maybe — I came because you're along."

He hadn't known he was going to say the last; it slipped unthinking off his tongue. She looked startled, for he saw her head lift and the dim glow from the fire enabled him to see her eyes. Her lips scarcely moved:

"You didn't say you saw how helpless we really are."

Martin picked up the buckets and as she turned with him, he said, "I wonder if I want to see, too."

Next morning Augustin and Sanford and Martin had the first two wagons ready, the teams harnessed and hooked up, before Witt brought his mules jangling in from watering. The man was either born lazy or a laggard by design, Martin concluded, watching him. He could appear to hurry, as he was this very moment, while making the least progress. Worse, the mules were growing fractious under his fumbling handling.

In exasperation, Martin helped Witt finish hooking up and the wagons rolled southwest.

Full daylight broke clear and keen, like a shutter opening on the endless rolling to hilly plains, vivid in toppings of reddish brown and yellow, drifting on the dark green sea of grass and its ever-present debris of blanched buffalo bones.

The sun stood at noon when Martin discovered the pocking of hoofs and the wide tracks of wagons coming in to the Double Mountain Fork and bearing up it southwest. The broad trail looked as if an army had passed.

Riding back, he halted the train and rode around to the rear of his wagon, where Burke's horse trailed on a halter rope. Burke occupied about the same flattened-out position he had at the start of the day, his hangdog eyes disconsolately on the canvas hood.

"Get up, Rip," Martin said. "Rise and shine." The cheerless eyes just stared at him. Burke didn't move. Martin said, "Time to hit the saddle."

"Any man who'd let his friends down," Burke moaned, condemning himself.

"You must figure you're big medicine," Martin rode him. "Hell, you're not the first man who got his snoot wet and made a jackass of himself." The listless shape on the blanket squirmed. "If you're waiting for me to say we need you, you won't hear it from me," Martin resumed. "We can always turn back." He turned the gelding a bit.

"Turn back?" Burke echoed. From the edge of his vision Martin saw him sit up.

"Have to if our Indian friend can't savvy my signs."

Burke pushed up on one elbow. "Reckon I could powwow with her a little, weak an' no good as I am," he said and groaned, hinting for sympathy.

Martin gave him none. "What good will it do? Trumbo's bunch is ahead of us. I just found their tracks coming in. We're whipped unless the old woman knows a short cut."

"Maybe," Burke said, scratching his thorny chin. His woebegone expression was weakening, his changeful face near its natural foxiness.

"You're in no shape to powwow."

Burke straightened ever so little. "Old Double Mountain Fork does a heap o' turnin' an' twistin' here on. Goes on southwest 'fore it kites off northwest. Maybe," he said in the tone of a man talking to himself, and he began crawling out of the wagon. His hands shook. He was weaving on his feet, but this time he held his head up as he went painfully toward the Sanfords' wagon.

The Indian woman looked weaker to Martin. The wrinkles inscribed deeper in her sunken cheeks, the smoky-black eyes dull with weariness. She sat up when she saw Burke wanted to talk, and in doing so she seemed smaller to Martin, drawn down to the husk of herself. The bright red ribbon which Harriet had arranged in the cropped, gray hair was like a badge for the will Martin saw living in the withered features. For Burke she showed a particular look of greeting that rose above their races, that said they shared images of the teeming prairie which no one would experience again. For himself Martin saw the fine old eyes warmly favoring him. He smiled back at her.

Instead of indulging in time-consuming ceremony and his bent for playing the actor, Burke opened up talking Comanche and framing signs. Martin saw her give a start, by which he knew Burke had told her that Trumbo's outfit of hunters was ahead of them; and he saw the flash of her eyes and afterward an ineffable emotion when she made the buffalo sign.

For the next minutes she and Burke inhabited a world of their own, apart in another time. Her sonorous Comanche crackled, in turn became rambling and reminiscing; her crabbed hands flew and sometimes they were as graceful ravels of smoke as she drew word-pictures. Once more she made the buffalo sign, after which she lay back on the pallet, exhausted, her mouth cupped. Through the poignancy of her eyes and face, she sent a meaning which transcended mere language and which Martin understood as though she had spoken to him in his own tongue: that the buffalo was of the spirit and meant life itself to her and her people, and she must find it before the Breathmaker came.

She was finished.

Burke and Martin stepped around to the front of the wagon with the Sanfords.

"She says leave the river," Burke told them. "Go straight west. We'll come to the river later. Go fast. She's mighty tired."

"This Medicine Place?" Sanford asked in eagerness. "How far is it?"

"Three, four days, she says."

"*She says — she says,*" Martin repeated roughly. "It was that far at Rath City, wasn't it? Is she out of her head?"

"I can't say she isn't," Sanford said thoughtfully, "but neither can I say she is.

She's going on will power alone."

"Tell you one thing," Burke retorted, with a flare of his old self, "if we don't git her there 'fore she dies, you sure as thunder won't see your bison, Doc."

In haste, Martin rode the south bank looking for a crossing. A buffalo trail, ancient and deep and steep and unused for some time, led to the stream. The men wielded shovels to widen it for passage of the wagons; finished, they made a sloping cut on the north bank.

Augustin started first. As the mules kicked up sprays of glistening water, he lashed the ends of the reins across their rumps and they lurched faster. About two rods and the wagon sank to the wheel hubs. Augustin, cussing in French, stood up and whipped the mules harder and shouted their names and they responded with a leather-snapping and jangling that jerked the wagon loose and safely across in a shower of mud and sand and brown water.

Sanford, sawing on the reins like a sulky driver, took his light wagon in next. Harriet gripped the wagon seat, her face beneath the flowered straw sailor hat showing a composed excitement. Sanford's progress was steady until he reached the place where Augustin had bogged down; here, too, his wagon sank to the hubs and here, too, he lashed his mules and they pulled the wagon across in a splatter of muddy water.

Martin turned in uncertainty as Witt drove the heavy wagon into the widened trail. Stepping fast, the six mules jingled down the incline and into the water. Witt wasn't forcing them. The mules began to lose momentum.

"Make 'em pull!" Martin shouted.

Almost languidly, Witt snapped the reins at the rear team, and it struck out faster, but not fast enough. The front wheels dropped to the hubs. Witt shouted and went to the reins again, whipping awkwardly and missing many of his lashes, and suddenly the nervous mules were floundering and confused and the wagon was bogged.

Martin spurred down the cut and saw Burke's mount hit the water on the other side at the same time. The mules were in a wild-eyed tangle, lunging this way and that, when Martin reached them. He grabbed the left leader's bridle bit and steadied him, leading him out straight. Burke was doing likewise on the right side.

Burke raised a warning shout. Martin glanced back, saw a rear mule down and struggling, head high. Martin cut back. Leaning low from the saddle, he seized the mule's bridle and pulled to help it up. The animal floundered and humped its back, fighting to stand. It couldn't, Martin saw then, because a rear leg was tangled in the leather trace.

He came down in the waist-high water, feeling the slippery mud and sand under his boots. He groped for the trace and found the chain-end, which he unhooked from the single tree; and while Burke kept the teams on a straight line, he tugged the trace clear of the mule's flailing leg and got the mule on its feet, and hooked the trace chain back on the single tree and climbed sloshing into the saddle and rode to the lead mule.

"Make 'em pull!" he yelled at Witt and led out.

Witt's awkward lethargy vanished. He was standing as he shouted and whipped the mules brutally and expertly. Crazy to leave so frightening a place, they surged against the wet harness while Martin and Burke pulled on the leaders. The wagon rocked and settled back. But the mules never quit. Witt punished them without letup. Everyone was shouting now. The mules humped lower and the wagon rocked and swayed, rose again, hung there a moment, snapped forward and in a rush the quick-footed mules were splashing and scrambling for the north bank. The firmer the footing the faster they moved, and they took the wagon racing up the cut, swinging from side to side.

As soon as Witt reached level ground and hauled up, Martin wheeled back to him. "Why'd you slow up?"

Save for splatters of sandy mud, Witt looked unchanged after the wild tussle. "Didn't figure it'd be that bad."

"Hell, you saw the other wagons bog down."

Not waiting for Witt's reply, Martin rode to his wagon and dismounted to take off his boots and pour out the water, reviewing Witt's carelessness as he tugged on the wet leather. On the other hand, Witt had handled the mules well during the pull-out.

Burke loped up, shivering and miserable after his wet ride. He gave a distinct cough and rubbed the flat of his hand over his chest. "If there's one thing that's the death of a man," he complained, "it's a bath in the spring of the year."

Martin felt a grin working on his mouth. Burke kept a serious mien. "All right, damnit," Martin gave in and took a bottle from the saddlebag, uncorked it and passed it up to Burke, who threw back his head for a long, gurgling drink. His Adam's apple bobbed like a boy's fishing cork. He brought the bottle down, blew through his oxbow mustache and swiped a sleeve across his moist mouth. "I God," he breathed gratefully, red-eyed, "I God," and he shot another sidewise longing at the bottle. Martin, foreseeing that, took it back.

After resting the teams, they rode out front and that was when Burke spotted the unshod hoofmarks and the deep scratches in the old trail which they now followed.

"Travois marks," Burke said. "Means women an' kids."

"Big bunch?"

" 'Bout like the one Mary scared off. Better keep your cannibal owl medicine bone handy."

Liking the smooth prairie footing after the treacherous crossing, the fast-stepping mules pulled the wagons at a constant clip. During midafternoon, while the first two wagons continued to roll, Martin saw Witt's teams hanging back and the gap widening between his vehicle and the others.

Wearily, Martin rode back.

Witt sat the seat like a sack of feed, indifferent and not indicating that he understood Martin's reason for having to halt the train.

"What's wrong?" Martin asked.

"That mule there's got a loose shoe, I reckon," Witt said, pointing a stubby hand. "Figured I'd see about it when we camped. Didn't want to slow us down."

"We'll see about it *now*," Martin said. "*Now*."

He waved for Augustin to drive back, and they took the mule out of the traces and pulled the shoe and nailed it on, and by that time half an hour was lost. Meanwhile, Witt stood around watching them handle the fractious animal.

Witt kept up during the rest of the afternoon, and at sundown they made dry camp, watered the stock from the barrels on the sides of the wagons and turned to picketing the stock for the night.

"In close this time," Martin called to the teamster. Witt gave no sign that he heard, but he picketed nearby.

Augustin's fire of buffalo chips was glowing. Mingling smells of coffee and bread and bacon drifted like essences on the twilight wind. Witt waited by his wagon for the supper call.

"Aren't you being a little harsh on Mr. Witt?" Harriet said.

More in surprise than annoyance, Martin explained about Indians running off stock at night and about the near loss of the wagon during the crossing, the one wagon needed for hauling the buffalo calves, and how the loose shoe, if not refitted, could have lamed a valuable mule.

"I guess he's doing the best he can," she said.

"That's the point — he knows better. Notice how he finally bullwhacked the teams across the fork? He's an old hand — when he wants to be."

"But why . . . ?" she began.

Augustin called supper and Witt tramped in and squatted down without greeting. He ate in great wolfing bites, maintaining an unbroken relay from tin plate to bearded mouth. In a few minutes he had finished. Rising, silent, he tramped back to the wagon.

"Friendly cuss," Burke observed.

"Ever seen him before?" Martin asked.

"Nope."

The moon lay waiting and the early prairie darkness was still warm like gossamer, when Martin decided to walk the picket line, more to check Witt's work, before Augustin started the first watch. He could see Witt sitting against a wagon wheel as he smoked a pipe. Martin passed him in silence, the man's presence like a claw in his back.

Harriet Sanford stood beside the light

wagon, facing the fragrant prairie. A firefly light glowed through the wagon hood, the faintness of Fielding Sanford's carefully shielded lantern by which he made notes each evening before retiring early. Thus Martin saw the slimness of her as she hugged the shawl about her, and the impression of contemplation in the rounded molding of her face, and also an awareness of him. She was waiting for him. He stopped.

"What will happen," she said, "if we reach the Medicine Place about the same time Trumbo does?"

"We couldn't stop him, if that's what you mean. He'd roll right over us if we tried. He'll wipe out the buffalo — if there are any buffalo."

She regarded him a moment before she spoke again. "You still don't believe her. You will never believe what you don't see hard and plain."

"Like I said, I'm willing to go see."

She seemed to consider that and she pulled the shawl tighter to her. He sensed her restlessness; together they strolled out over the dim prairie.

"Why — why would they wipe out everything?" She sounded bewildered. "Just for money?"

"Money's not all of it, though the market's high." Knowing why, he thought, was easy. "It's like a drunk who's finished off all the whisky in camp and stumbles onto a bottle somebody hid. He's gonna have that, too. One last, glorious spree. Who cares this late?"

"You seem to know Trumbo's men."

"He and I were friends once. Except for some things, I could be one of them."

"Was it . . . a woman who caused you to give up hunting?"

Her perception gave him a small start. "That was the main reason," he admitted, "and a woman has helped bring me back to it. I've come full circle after all these years. Some time I'll tell you about it."

"And her?"

"Her, too."

"I ought not to have pried," she said, strolling on through the filmy night. By now they were some distance out. Looking back, he couldn't make out the tiny glow of Sanford's wagon.

"We've gone far enough," Martin said. It wasn't an order. Nor spoken in alarm. A weblike quality overspread the night. Distance meant nothing. He had the light-headed feeling that they could walk endlessly like this together and never tire.

"Why?" She paused and her tone was teasing.

"Didn't I tell you? Indians like to skulk around wagons at night."

"They do?" She spoke carelessly and went on faster, in long, graceful steps.

Because she was obviously enjoying herself, he let her proceed. But after several rods, when he saw she was going much farther, he took her arm for the first time, lightly. She ignored him. She seemed to be drifting in thought under the pale sky.

His firm pull swung her around and in to him. He felt his hands touch her arms, then go around her. He glimpsed the paleness of her face turning to him just before he kissed her and felt the velvet of her body. Her lips, firmly tentative in the beginning, softened to warm responsiveness. She barely drew her head back.

"Harriet," he said, "that's something for a man to believe."

She drew farther away. "Why?" Her voice had a curious directness.

"Because I felt it. It was right, it was true. I know." He reached for her again. She stayed motionless. He let his hands drop, knowing the moment was broken.

She said, "You *felt* it, yes. You didn't have to see it like a mountain or a wall."

"I see you — you're real," he said, baffled by her tone, and then he understood and he said, "You let me kiss you to prove a point, didn't you?" He went on before she could speak. "You remind me of do-gooders I saw in Kansas among the Kaws, so-called missionaries preaching brotherhood while thieving white settlers camped on Indian land. Well, don't try to convert me."

Even though he couldn't see her face clearly, he saw the flinching jerk of her body.

"Martin," she said and she came in and touched his arm, "you must have faith in someone besides yourself. You must believe in others when they tell you the truth. Everything's not just flesh and blood."

"Don't waste your breath. Right now I'm not fair game for a female missionary among the heathen Comanches."

She stiffened away from him. She tossed her head and swept past him in a swish of long skirts, saying:

"Don't be so sure you felt anything — anything at all. I didn't!"

Lying in the wagon, Martin heard Burke, who was standing Augustin's watch, come in and Sanford go out to take the second tour. Martin kept dozing off from time to time, never fully asleep. His head was too

253

full of restless turnings. He distrusted the situation into which they were moving, at the direction of a savage ancient who was in and out of her mind, yet shrewd enough to use sympathetic white people to carry through her whims.

Harriet's face came before his eyes and he recalled exactly how her voice sounded, both earnest and nettling. What had happened to them tonight? For a little everything was right, he knew, but soon over, like the flash of black gunpowder on the rise as the enraged bull charged Trumbo.

Lulled by the steady grass-cropping of the grazing stock, he dozed again. Later, he heard Sanford's quiet steps across the grass to Witt's wagon, followed presently by Witt's heavier tread along the picket line. Witt was scheduled to awaken Martin at three o'clock for the last watch. The bootsteps faded and Martin sank into a light sleep.

A touch of cold in the prairie night, a subtle wrongness. Martin sat up in vague alarm. Fleetingly, as his eyes opened on the dull gray ceiling of the wagon top, he thought he was camped at Trumbo's hide quarters or on the Clear Fork at Griffin. He had no idea how long he had been dozing. He shook his head, disturbed and not knowing why. He struck a match and shielded the light. His watch read: two-thirty. His senses were sharper now. He could hear his horse moving near the wagon, but he heard neither the soft croppings nor the muffled stampings of the other picketed animals. The absence of these sounds had aroused him. He pulled on his boots, took the handgun and slipped outside, still hearing no more than the movements of his mount. A sallow moon rode the sky.

His sinking uneasiness intensified as the silence continued to hang. He was thinking of Indians when he prowled past the wagon and looked up and down, searching the leaden light. Augustin's mules were gone. Feeling in the short grass, he found a cut picket rope; and another. Witt? Where was he? Walking faster, Martin approached the wagon which Witt drove. No mules grazed there and he hurried on toward the Sanford wagon.

He halted, head cocked to the slow tap of hoofs brushing through the grass. He saw what looked like a saddle horse, yes — Sanford's, and a figure leading it. At the same moment the figure discovered him, and he saw blurred motion and spurting flame before he pulled the trigger and felt the pistol jump in his hand. He fired again, quickly, and heard a cry.

He swung about, expecting a rush of

whooping figures across the open prairie upon the wagons. None came. Not a single sound followed. He ran. A shape writhed on the ground. A white man. It was Witt. Martin searched the grass and found Witt's pistol. He heard voices; he called for someone to bring a lantern.

Sanford, it was, who rushed up with the light, a step ahead of the rest. Witt's face looked ugly and pasty with sweat. He groaned. His breathing was jerky. But his eyes blazed.

"You're with Trumbo," Martin said. "Speak up."

"Go t'hell."

Witt's clenched teeth were like solid yellow pegs bracing the brown-bearded face, contorted in pain, sullen even now. Witt was dying for Trumbo, willing to die, defending Trumbo, as Martin had for too long.

"I remember now," Martin said. "You were in Trumbo's camp the day I rode in."

Witt gasped. He couldn't speak.

Martin stood away from him. Sanford knelt over Witt and opened his shirt. He looked a moment, drew the shirt together and rose, shaking his head.

Harriet Sanford pressed a hand to her throat. "It's terrible. Poor Mr. Witt."

Martin didn't spare her feelings. "*Poor Mr.*

Witt cut the mules loose. No telling where they are. He was going to steal your father's horse. And he shot at me first."

"I see," she said in a changed voice.

"I don't think you do. This is just the start."

Chapter 11

Martin and Burke spent most of the morning rounding up the mules and driving them to the train. Now the glassy sun was drawing a bead on the middle of the afternoon. With half a day lost, Martin could no more than wonder where Trumbo's outfit might be following the Double Mountain Fork. If Trumbo had riders scouting ahead of his wagons and skinners, then the horsemen would reach the Medicine Place before Sanford possibly could.

A wryness knitted the corners of his mouth. If such a place actually existed near the fork, if there were any buffalo.

In rolling country empty of life, the eye was quick to notice any movement, whether antelope, wolf or vulture. When Martin spotted the roll of dust far to the rear, he thought first of Trumbo or Indians and he dropped behind to watch.

Shortly the dust developed into a small knot of horsemen. Two riders. In a hurry.

Burke loped back, laid a squinting appraisal on the rear and shook his head in a puzzled way. "White men," he said, as though Indians were more predictable. "There's a handy place up ahead to make a stand, in case there's more behind them two."

Martin saw a broken elevation, the shattered tail of an eroded ridge line, ribbed with an outcrop of red rocks, where a man could see in all directions. He formed the wagons in a crescent, the open end against the rocks, and the men unhitched and led the stock inside. Burke posted himself on the hump overlooking the wagons, and Martin loaded the Sharps and waited by the center vehicle.

When the riders were yet a mile away, he raised the sights and dropped a bullet in front of them. Just two men. No one in sight behind them. They shrank back at the shot, but did not scatter or circle. Neither did they act afraid. In a moment he was surprised to see them waving their hats. Once more they started along the train's trail.

For good measure, Martin boomed another slug short. This time they fanned out wider. Again they came ahead, waving hats.

He let them close within two hundred

yards. He fired the next shot over their heads. They halted and one man rode forward, holding his hat high.

At fifty yards Martin saw, wonderingly, that it was Kyle, Ruby Hillyard's right-hand man. Kyle halted, waiting for a sign to come in.

Martin's suspicions jumped and he called up to Burke to look all around. When Burke said he saw no others, Martin signaled Kyle forward.

Kyle turned to wave in his companion. Martin's shout stopped him, "Just you — Kyle — just you!"

Kyle's arm dropped. He hesitated and heeled his horse ahead.

Watching, Martin found himself holding no sharply defined opinion of the man. Loyal, yes; unexcitable and no doubt enduring and thick-skinned since he worked for Miss Ruby. Martin searched for a closer assessment. Ruby knew men. She wasn't one to tolerate inefficiency; therefore, Kyle had to be capable. Defeat was inconceivable to her; so Kyle got her what she demanded, did in his plodding, unimaginative way.

A new wariness affected Martin, a certain respect for the plain-faced man riding up to the wagons, while he waited for Kyle to state his business.

"Miss Ruby sent us to help you," Kyle said. His voice was flat, wrung dry of emotion.

"Help us what?"

"Why, to ketch them buffalo."

"What buffalo?"

Kyle's heavy mouth wrinkled slightly, the closest Martin had seen him to a grin. "Everybody in Rath knows what you're after. Miss Ruby was right. She said it'd be hard to convince you she wants to help." He was a patient man, a dogged one.

"Is," Martin said, "when she's in with Trumbo."

"You're wrong. She gave Sid his walkin' papers."

Sanford was listening, intent on every word. Harriet came over to stand by her father. Kyle touched the brim of his hat to her, a courtesy that seemed more mechanical than inspired politeness. A hard-won result, Martin guessed, of Miss Ruby's hand-reining.

"Just had an evil thought," Martin said. "You're here to see we don't scare off any buffalo before Trumbo's crew cleans 'em out."

A match-point flame struck in Kyle's gray eyes and sparked out. He had, Martin discerned, learned to curb his temper.

"Two of us?" Kyle answered, and there was logic in that, Martin admitted to himself. "Tell you what," Kyle said, trudging on. "You can keep our guns till you say we can have 'em back." He unbuckled his gun belt and pulled his saddle gun and held them out.

Martin did not move. He met Sanford's eye and stepped back out of Kyle's hearing.

"I know I was wrong about Witt," Sanford said. "But why would these men give up their arms if they meant harm?"

"There's a catch in it somewhere," Martin said, thinking of Ruby Hillyard. Was he misjudging her?

"I don't understand." Sanford's eyes were as innocence itself, the mirror of a man without duplicity; hence, he could not detect it in others.

Martin attempted to tell him in a few words. He quit suddenly. Some circumstances could not be explained when there were no real answers. When a friend changed? When a lonely woman compromised, desperate for the security she'd never have? Martin couldn't. He didn't want to try.

"We're short of men, Martin. If you keep their guns, they can't harm us."

Martin could see that. Trumbo had thirty

men at least. For Sanford to capture enough calves, he had to reach the buffalo first and work fast. There wouldn't be much time. If Trumbo got there first, violence would result if Sanford tried to take calves. It was a general rule on the buffalo range that the outfit locating a herd had priority; no man disturbed a herd that was being shot out. Time counted. Two extra men would help. Martin could see these plain factors. But how far did Miss Ruby's break with Trumbo go? Was it real?

"Martin," Sanford insisted, displaying his most appealing manner, "I feel we have no choice. We have to let Kyle join us."

"It *is* your expedition," Martin conceded. "All right." He returned to Kyle. "There are two conditions. We search both of you for other weapons." He expected Kyle's protest. Kyle nodded agreement and Martin finished: "You place yourselves under our orders."

"We came to help," Kyle replied agreeably. "You can search me now."

Kyle and the other man carried no concealed weapons and Martin deposited their gunbelts and saddle guns in his wagon and the train resumed its journey.

It was nearly an hour later when Augustin, in the lead, balked at traversing a rough draw.

The two Hillyard riders dismounted and used shovels and dug out rocks, and pushed and heaved on each successive wagon while Martin and Burke, attaching ropes, urged their horses up the steep places.

Martin's doubts grew smaller. The two extra men had helped save the train half an hour or more.

That night as a precaution against repeating the mistake he had with Witt, he decided not to leave the new men on guard alone. And so he paired each of them with Burke and himself. The night passed without incident.

After daylight Martin and Burke and Sanford agreed it would be wise for the hunter to ride south for the Double Mountain Fork and locate Trumbo's trail. As Burke finished saddling, he fixed thirsty eyes on Martin's saddlebag.

"Medicine's no good if you don't take it regular," he observed, his lower lip pouting.

"Help yourself, Rip." Martin was tightening his saddle cinch. From the rim of his eye he saw Burke take his long, gurgling "toddy," wipe his mouth and blow, stand a moment in struggle with himself, then hammer the cork home, using the heel of his hand, and almost reverently return the bottle to the bag.

He caught up at noon, his mustang as light-footed as at daybreak. Burke looked dusty and cantankerous.

"Trumbo's due south of us," he reported. "We'd better hump it."

A sense of order prevailed throughout the afternoon, and the train covered the farthest distance of the journey in one day. The next day found the wagons rolling steadily, breasting one treeless swell of land after another, no buffalo in sight and scarcely any swift, white-rumped antelope. The prairie brimmed with a flood of glittering yellow light. The smell of the grass was sweet, and the constant wind, while hot, felt cool under the canvas of the wagon tops. The grain-fed mules kept stepping fast, long ears twitching, eyes alert, eager to see more of the wide-open world around them.

Martin became conscious of a gradual change. He no longer saw fields of bleached buffalo bones spoiling the verdure of spring. For miles he had not. Hunters seemed to have observed an invisible boundary and not ventured beyond. Martin thought again of Indians, and in the fascination of the appealing distances promptly forgot them. The land lay clean and fresh under the sparkling sky, natural and untouched after the waste behind them, inviting the eye to look just over the next green rise for shaggy life grazing the short grass; if not there, the next rise or the next.

Harriet Sanford halted the team and signaled. Anxious signals, Martin thought, and he wondered if the old woman was worse. Riding back with Burke, he saw the Comanche woman drawn up on the seat beside Harriet, perched there like an exhausted bird. Warm as the day was, she clutched a woolen blanket, wiveled, stooped, more weary than yesterday, the skin on her face like cracked leather. But her smoky eyes gleamed. She shrilled Comanche at Burke, extended her hands and turned them rapidly, again and again, and pointed.

Burke peered westward and said to Martin: "She says go faster. Breathmaker's comin' soon enough. Water's not far ahead. There's a crossing." He drove his voice at Martin. Solemnity, not raffishness, filled his face. "She says don't stop. Not till we come to the Medicine Place."

"Ask her how we'll know it." Martin's doubts crept into his tone, for she was being vague again.

As if miffed that Martin should question her judgment, Burke cut a jerky sign and muttered in Comanche. Her high, scolding voice fairly crackled in return.

"She says no more time for talk. You'll know it when you see it."

"I hope so. Rip, you better tail out to the crossing. See what's there."

Everything was too hazy for Martin's liking. Too much like an old woman's caprice. Was she cunningly promising one thing to cover up another, hinting about buffalo and a mysterious place in order to hide her determination to see her people once more, to die near them?

He looked at her in question, and caught her in the act of bestowing her favor upon him. A divided favor at the moment. For in the ancient countenance he saw an undisguised longing, and a dreaming, as she looked upon the heaving land.

There was no doubt or hesitation in Harriet's manner. She slapped the reins and the mules stepped out. Burke was quirting away. Martin glanced behind him. Kyle and the other rider were there. He had almost forgotten them. He hastened ahead to lead the way.

The treeless footing dipped and climbed and wound around, piling up rougher, forcing Martin to lead the train left and right to find gentler grades. When in doubt, he asked the old woman, in signs, and unvaryingly she pointed without hesitating.

His flounderings seemed to entertain her. He lost track of time.

He gaped, unprepared for the streaky shine of water bending away like a piece of sheeny ribbon — the Double Mountain Fork — which he had figured lay miles yet to the northwest.

And he thought: So the old woman knew.

And before long, descending into the valley of the fork, he was riding upon an ancient passageway leading to water. He could sense its swarming past. A broad crossing for restless buffalo herds and for war parties helling for the lower Texas settlements and Old Mexico, over the ages worn by countless hoofs, down through sandy loam to the packed underside of trampled yellowish clay. Now bearing recent travois marks.

She knew exactly, he thought.

Impatient for the wagons to catch up, he looked back and realized his unconscious haste. He rode into the water, paused for his horse to drink, and going on felt solid bottom come under the gelding and stay solid to the south bank.

Burke was dusting up in a high lope.

Waiting, Martin scanned the ground beyond the crossing. A worn trail, winding with the stream, twisted dimly away to the northwest. He was relieved to find no wagon rim marks. No shod hoofprints. The ones he saw were unshod and not today's, mingling with the travois scratches turning up the fork.

"We're ahead of Trumbo," Martin shouted. "We beat him!"

"Damn little," Burke answered and bent a hard eye southeast. "I saw dust a few miles back. He's comin'!"

A few miles. That meant about an hour's lead, Martin estimated. No more. Maybe less. He rode to the bank and waved for everyone to hurry.

Augustin shouted. His mules raised dripping muzzles and he lashed them into action, across and up the clay bank. Harriet's lively team followed without mishap, and Sanford brought the heavy wagon handily across. Kyle and the other Hillyard hand crossed.

When Martin told him the news about Trumbo, Sanford seemed to realize for the first time what might happen.

"I want no violence, Martin."

"You know I can't promise that."

"I forbid any violence. You must avoid it."

Martin chewed on his lower lip, a hot impatience driving through him. He let it recede. Sanford's gentle nature and training simply precluded the use of physical violence toward an end. Martin left him to ride to Burke, yelling, "Now where? Ask her."

They rode to Harriet's wagon, and forthwith the old Indian woman, clinging to her wagon-seat perch, hurled a splatter of Comanche instructions and lifted the gnarled roots of her hands. Fluently, briefly they spoke: *Northwest. Hurry.* She lay back then, her life-weary face toward the slipping sun, her crinkled mouth open like a tired bird's.

In spite of his doubts, Martin could sense an unhesitating direction. Twice during the next hour he told Burke to ask the way. And each time she replied in a twinkling and lay down on the seat more exhausted than before, and each time they followed her directions, always toiling within sight of the fork. Once Martin saw Harriet point to the pallet on the floor of the wagon. With a slight shake of her head, the old one shut her eyes and opened them and signed for *Hurry. Heap hurry.*

Martin scowled at the choppy country into which they were moving. Forbidding, empty, harsh. Cover for a hundred war parties. He stabbed Burke an inquiring look and got nothing. Burke rode at ease, yet obsessed with the roughness ahead. At the rear the two Hillyard men rode, content to follow in the pall of yellow dust raked up by the wagons.

Martin's eyes strayed again to the blanketed figure on the wagon seat and he knew both pity and doubt. Was she merely obeying old instincts and listening to memories, remembering old trails and trusted crossings — the country as it was in the prime of her life, when her husband and sons lived and she cared for them? Was she, in the dreaming of her wandering mind, leading them nowhere?

They began ascending a rock-pitted slope, the wagon frames groaning and creaking, the teams straining, heads down. Up here the country rolled away to infinity, broken along the course of the Double Mountain Fork, smoothing and rippling beyond it. Not a single wild animal in sight.

He looked back the way they had traveled, and felt a cold flinch. Dust ruffled the trail down there. The dust of Trumbo's wagons, a sinuous snake of wagons and horsemen writhing with the stream. And closer than he had figured. Far closer.

He spurred ahead to tell Burke. He saw Burke, who was riding point, reach the crest and halt. In that instant rider and horse became frozen images.

Martin came beside him. The air was hot and still. He looked.

One rounded mound jutted out of the

plain below, weird in the dancing glitter of afternoon heat, strange and portentous in its solitary aloofness, in its shimmering nimbus of glazy vapor, its flat cap rock remindful of a pyre, its starkness multiplied by the surrounding emptiness.

A feeling opened in Martin: the Medicine Place.

Burke turned his face and Martin saw not his own astonishment matched there. Instead, Burke's look of triumph, like a sneer. Because old Rip Burke, drunkard, braggart, liar, cheat, whatever, had believed from the beginning and Martin had not till this moment.

Chapter 12

Burke touched spurs, the shoes of his horse clicking on the rock litter as he spurred downward for the plain.

Martin, holding up for the wagons, saw Augustin begin the descent, foot braced on the brake lever, the heavy rub blocks screeching against the rims.

Harriet's light wagon swayed up the long grade, the heads of the spirited mules bobbing. The old Indian woman was sitting rigidly upright. She knew just where to look. At the exact moment the wagon reached the top, the dreaming spread over her face and transformed it, like a sudden light, and still possessed it when Harriet, obeying Martin's hurry-on motion, started down. He rode in alongside the team. Behind him Sanford's wagon bumped up the slope.

At the bottom Martin reformed the wagons, Harriet's in front, the easier to watch the old one's directions, then the calf wagon and Augustin in the rear.

Dust fumed up from the wagon wheels in choking brown clouds as the train strung out to cross the plain. On Martin's left the mound rose several hundred feet, as mysterious at ground level as above, brooding, secure in solitude, defying the erosion of time, changing color as the wagons hurried by, glinting flashes of reds and yellows and dulling to somber browns.

Rounding the other side of the mound, Martin searched across the plain and saw further emptiness. He fixed his discouragement on a ridge which tailed off northwest, as high as the one they had last come over. His doubts struck back. There was no life here, none at all; only the hazy images in the dreams of a dying old woman.

Burke looked uncertain, too. He hitched

around in the saddle for instructions. She was ready and watching, as if expecting them to falter. Her brown hands clawed: *Go around the ridge. Go fast.*

Onward a little farther Martin noticed the first buffalo wallows seen south of the fork, huge saucer-shaped depressions, dry as bone; but the droppings he saw were old. Was it his imagination? Did the short grass, which was beginning to take on the greenish gray of early summer, look thicker and richer? It seemed so.

They rode to the sloping tail of the ridge, swung to go around as the old woman had told them. Nearby, his eyes found the same void which he had passed, another stretch of lifeless plain. But when he raised the sights of his eyes and looked away, he grew still and straight, not believing his own senses.

The plain was teeming, black with life. Not a vast herd as in the early days, everywhere as far as the eye could see across the prairie sea. Yet many buffalo. Heap buffalo. Hundreds in little bunches. Grazing the tufted grass, shaggy heads pointed into the southwest, into the wind as always, away from the train. Newborn calves, not old enough for their humps to show, their coats bright yellow or tawny. Their mothers looking protective and savage and alert, their dark winter coats hanging in patches. Gazing that distance, he felt a sensation of dreaminess. Did he really see them? Was he imagining them? Since he knew how buffalo looked during the calving season, was his mind playing him tricks?

Burke was speechless. He kept straining forward, grizzled mouth ajar.

Sanford jumped down from the wagon and ran up, a kindling elation ablaze in his eyes. "What did I tell you! What did I tell you! Just as she said!"

The three of them looked again, as though to remind themselves the buffalo were still there.

"We can't drive 'em," Martin said. "Maybe we can drift a little bunch."

"You can't drift buff'lo," Burke snarled. "I God, you can't!"

"By God, we can try. See where the plain breaks up toward the fork? Looks like the head of a big gully or canyon. We could start drifting a bunch into that, where we can handle a few."

Burke gave a violent shake of his head. "Be better to shoot some cows out here. Cut out the calves on horseback."

"We'd spook the whole herd. Hell, no, Rip."

"Have to shoot the cows if you take their

calves. I God, you know that."

"Not necessarily," Martin said and realized they were talking in terse spurts, on edge, suddenly divided and thereby wasting time, afraid to make a bold move lest it be wrong.

Sanford's reasonable voice wedged tempering between them. "We haven't much choice. I believe we can work around to that gully without disturbing them. They're grazing away from us. Once we get over there we'll know what to do."

He was striding for his wagon.

After turning the end of the ridge, Martin and Burke led to the right and, after going some distance parallel to the ridge, angled southwest, a course which placed the grazing black mass on their left. Off west ran the slim shine of the fork.

Martin watched the buffalo in fascination. So far they seemed unaware of intruders, or uncaring, he thought. It was evident they hadn't been shot into lately, unless Indians had hunted the fringes in a quiet way. The afternoon was hot, sluggish and stupefying. Just lazy-right, he saw, for a creeping hunter to manage a stand. Some animals were lying down. Some standing looked asleep. A tremendous bull on the rim of the herd raised his massive head and gazed directly at Martin, who checked the walking gelding, fearful the bull would bolt and stampede the whole herd. Behind him Martin heard the wagons stop.

With relief, he saw the bull lower its head and recommence grazing. Only then did Martin ease the horse into a cautious walk.

Ahead he saw the reddish scar of the gully or wash or small canyon. What it really was, he saw now, was a buffalo trail whose beginning belonged to times long past. So eroded and gashed and gullied by water and wind that it looked abandoned. It dropped away and widened into a crooked canyon draining toward the fork.

He rode in closer and looked down, seeing the narrow, winding floor of the passage. Scrub cedars clung to the rocky sides and climbed in ragged clumps above the rim, dotting the jumbled brokenness on the other side. These were the breaks of the Double Mountain Fork, sheltered and remote from the white man, offering wood, water, and game.

Sanford's Elysium.

That crossed Martin's mind as he tracked his gaze up and down the shallow canyon. Men on horseback could bunch the buffalo at this end . . . Rope the little calves . . . Drag them up the trail . . . Tie them down for loading in the big wagon . . . The savage mother cows? They'd have to be shot, cruel and wasteful as it was. But you shot the old ones so the young ones could live. That made hard sense.

Excitement burned his throat. A swift conviction seized him. They could do it; they could. By God, they could. The rub was driving or drifting buffalo down there. If not, they'd try Burke's direct way after all. They'd have to.

He heard voices approaching and he saw Burke and Sanford, the latter puffing from his short run and the excitement. "We can do it," Martin said. "We've got to hurry."

"I want five heifer calves," Sanford told him, his voice near trembling, "— and three little fellows. That way —" He ceased to stare at something behind Martin.

Turning fast, Martin saw a sliding movement among the stubby cedars on the other side of the canyon. An Indian, naked from the waist up, stepped into plain view. He stared at the white men, as startled as they. He vanished almost as soon as Martin saw him, melting into the cedars. For another suspended moment, farther on, Martin saw the blur of a running figure and then he saw nothing. Meaning seemed to burrow and pile through him as he whipped around:

"She's got people camped in the breaks. That's why she wanted to come. It wasn't the buffalo."

Harriet's voice carried sharply above the stifling quiet. She was standing by the wagon. Calling, Martin saw, not for them but for the old woman. Martin followed Harriet's eyes, turned also by a sense. The old one was wobbling in the direction of the buffalo.

Harriet called again and ran after her. Without pausing, the old woman glanced back and flung up a clawlike hand and motioned away and hastened on. It was curious to see how Harriet obeyed. Not in fear, not in understanding; but affected by an acuteness keener than reason that said it would be wrong to stop her.

Likewise, Martin's impulse to ride out left him, forgotten when the old woman turned her face to the sky and raised her arms and uttered a high wailing. It chilled him. It rose on weird tones out of the primitive ages — *ahhh-ahhh*. A singing that wasn't a song. Tuneless. Yet Martin felt its impelling effect. He only watched now and wondered, back in the strange dreaminess.

She shuffled along, too weak to walk. The rawhide soles of her moccasins scuffed the short grass in feathery steps. At times she swayed and tottered and at times she paused for strength. But her high-pitched wailing never ceased.

Martin sensed a different cry. Was she calling the buffalo in her unhurried, knowing way?

The nearest bunch of buffalo grazed without apparent notice of the approaching figure. Her voice dropped to a low chant. Martin could barely hear it now. The wind caught her cropped gray hair, giving her a spectral wildness. Her long buckskin dress was a muted yellow against the plain of dark, humped beasts. The chanting changed to a keen wailing. Indeed a calling now.

So gradual were her shuffling movements that a moment went by before Martin realized she stood by the ancient buffalo trail leading into the gully-washed canyon.

Distinctly now he heard her *ahh-ing* voice. It rose more shrill and somehow different. Was that a bleating?

Baleful and curious, a magnificent buffalo bull looked up. Then a cow. The tawny calf at her side stood as still and solemn as a child. The rhythm of the *ahhh-ing* came faster.

While Martin watched, the bull took a lumbering step, but no more. The cow stirred and suddenly the calf huddled at her flank. *Ahhh-ahhh.* Huge, mighty, the bull moved his bulk forward in plodding steps. His black chin-mop almost touched the grass. Behind him followed the cow and her calf.

Martin saw a perceptible quiver ripple through the other animals. It was like a small wave. And, in unison, all the buffalo began a lumbering drift toward the ancient trail and the waiting old woman. Her voice continued to call them, her *ahhh-ahhh* shrillness strangely gentle; and their hoofs made a rustling in the curly grass as of wind rising over the plain.

The great bull, fearless, scornful, hardly hesitated before the worn-down trail. His enormous head rocked as he descended, his thick body pitching. The band followed him in a clattering rush. A haze of reddish dust spread over the trail, partly obscuring the hurrying dark beasts. A rumbling started to sound below in the canyon's depths.

Martin's head cleared. He hadn't figured on the bull. "Rip — shoot that bull or any cow straying down the canyon."

Burke didn't move. His eyes rolled in warning. Martin turned and saw Kyle covering them from behind. A dismal Augustin stood between them and Kyle.

"Just took what was mine," Kyle said, waggling a pistol. "While Frenchy watched the buffalo show."

"Why this?"

"So you won't scare off the last buffalo herd in Texas. There's thousands of dollars out there. Miss Ruby wouldn't like that."

Miss Ruby. Martin understood in a sickening flash. But Kyle was alone. "Where's your pardner?"

"Dropped him off at that last ridge we came up," Kyle said, letting the rest dangle.

A hemmed-in feeling beset Martin. Back there, engrossed with the mound and then the buffalo, he'd completely forgotten Kyle. And suddenly he was seeing other shapes.

"To hurry up Trumbo?" Martin said and saw that affirmed in Kyle's face. "You let us lead you here, in case Trumbo missed the buffalo. And Trumbo sent Witt to slow us down so we wouldn't get too far ahead."

"You figure right good."

He could hear a milling in the canyon, and deep, guttural grunts. Everything sounded fainter, farther down the canyon. In a few minutes the buffalo would find their way out to the fork.

"All we want is those calves," Martin said.

Kyle ignored him. His attention was split, half covering them and half watching the plain where the herd grazed undisturbed into the wind.

Martin saw why. Past the buffalo, where the ridge slanted down to the prairie, he could see the scudding shapes of horsemen coming fast and fanning out. Some already dismounting and running ahead, lugging rifles and sacks of shells. Within three hundred yards they would set up rest sticks and commence firing. And when the Sharps started booming, the handful of buffalo in the canyon would flee.

A single hunter caught his eye. He rode in advance of the others, in the manner of a man who liked his ease. A hunter astride a buckskin, riding in as close to the herd as he dared. Trumbo. *Going to make it big again.* Trumbo and Ruby. They'd played him like a fiddle from the day of his arrival in Griffin.

These sensations tumbled through Martin in moments.

Kyle's voice hardened. "Get down."

"I said all we want is those calves," Martin argued. "We've got to plug the canyon now or they'll be gone." He was straining for reason. "Anyway, Trumbo'll start blasting in a minute."

"Miss Ruby says *you* get nothin'."

Fielding Sanford's frustration was painful for Martin to watch. He regarded Kyle in bewilderment, incapable of comprehending Kyle's actions, all the while seeming to look through the shards of a broken dream. He shook his head, baffled. He turned, listening to the lessening sounds in the canyon. At that his normally mild expression faded. He straightened and settled his lips and pulled on the brim of his dinky little eastern hat. He was going after Kyle with his bare hands.

Kyle saw, too, in disbelief, for such was not only foolhardy, but contrary to all the rules, something only a greener would attempt. A lamb fighting a wolf.

Sanford, his face grave and pale, stepped out. Kyle stared at him blankly another moment, yet ready to fire.

Martin kicked the gelding forward, drawing his pistol as he did. He heard the thud of horseflesh and felt the solid jar of the gelding's forequarters smashing Kyle's mount. Kyle was thrown across the withers of his horse, nearly out of the saddle. With a violent lurch, he righted himself and struggled to bring his pistol to bear on Martin.

Martin's bullet smashed him coming up, high on the chest. Kyle's shirt puffed dust. He let out an, "Ah —" He swayed, falling, shock clutching his square face. His wall-eyed horse was whirling. Kyle's head and shoulders thumped the ground and he lost his hat. His right foot was hanging in the stirrup when his horse bolted toward the fork.

"Rip" — Martin hurried — "watch the canyon."

Martin's eyes followed the runaway a bit longer, drawn to Kyle's loose body twisting and skimming over the grassy earth. Martin darted a look at the plain. Trumbo's buckskin was standing. A shot banged. But it wasn't a Sharps. It sounded behind Martin, slapping again before Martin could look.

It was Burke, down the canyon a way, and he saw Burke, on the canyon's rim, turn and hold his carbine over his head with both hands, signaling Done.

Martin spurred to go to him and, instead, pulled around, arrested by an unbelievable ringing and clanging. Did he hear bells? He did, distinctly. Among the buffalo. At the same instant he saw Indians riding full speed, dragging bells and shaking what resembled dried buffalo robes, yelling like demons as they rode into the herd.

Across the canyon wriggled a disorderly line of riders of drawn travois poles raising dust. Of women and children and old men quirting ponies. In their hasty flight some were throwing objects away, leaving a wake of litter.

A peculiar throbbing shook the prairie. Buffalo milled and grunted and scampered here and there, headlong, mad with fright, running in a blind, scattering rush. As the dreadful riders pressed after them, the confused animals swerved eastward, bunching up, running faster, crowding, a rumbling suction which swept other buffalo with them, more and more, until Martin saw a black wave pouring over the plain toward the dismounted hunters, their figures dim through the rising fog of dust.

Heavy rifles boomed, faint against the drumming roll. Erratic spats. The scattered firing dropped off.

Martin marked the buckskin horse. Trumbo was running for it. His long strides carried him along. He seemed about to reach his mount. That was the last Martin saw before the black mass thundered over him and the buckskin ran flying with the herd leaders.

Some hunters — those farther back along the line — were reaching their horses in time and flinging up and riding like humped jockeys ahead of the stampede or among the lead bunches. Other hunters, like Trumbo, couldn't make it; their riderless mounts, stirrups flapping, fled before the buffalo struck. And as the herd rolled on a curving, shifting course, it left rumpled figures scattered over the plain. One or two staggered up, took a few faltering steps and collapsed.

Already the din was dying. The Indian noise-makers were riding southwest to join their families fleeing the sanctuary of the cedar breaks.

With a start, Martin remembered the old woman. He looked around. She wasn't standing by the beaten-out trail. Nor by the wagons. He rode to the buffalo trace and looked down it toward the canyon, listening to the milling and grunting.

He didn't see the slight figure at first, so perfectly did her buckskin dress blend in color with the pulverized earth. She lay on her side in the thick dust, which still smelled of the wild scents of the shaggy beasts. Lightly, Martin saw, like a little brown leaf that had fluttered to the ground. A hint of dreaming yet on her face.

He was touched, but he felt no great ache of sorrow for her. He was glad for her instead. For she had lived by and vanished with the buffalo. She was brave.

And it was the buffalo after all. It was.

He heard a sound and discovered the Sanfords. They looked on in silence. Harriet's eyes were wet when she turned to him.

"Martin, she loved you like a son. Can you believe her now?"

For an answer, he dismounted and started along the trace.

Soon afterward, thinking of other things, Martin left the wagons and rode slowly toward the widening plain.

He found Trumbo lying face down. He groaned as Martin turned him over on his back. Martin drew back. Dust powdered Trumbo's tangled yellow hair, and his misshapen face looked not so much like a face as it did of ill-fitting parts grotesquely connected. His breathing was a broken hiss.

"Sid," Martin said; louder: "Sid."

The eyelids opened, then shut. Martin spoke his name again. The eyes struggled, opening, in them a dull response.

"It's Martin."

The crushed mouth stirred. A hollow croaking fell from it.

"Don't try to talk," Martin said. "I'll go get the wagon." It came to him that he hadn't expected to find Trumbo alive.

Trumbo reached out a staying hand; it had no strength. He was moaning and swallowing. The ruined mouth opened. Martin caught a hoarse word. Two words. The same words mumbled over. He couldn't make them out and he bent closer. Trumbo struggled, again forcing the hollow croakings.

Martin leaned back, unable to understand.

Desperation bulged in Trumbo's eyes. His odd, hoarse voice whispered: ". . . not true."

The strangest of sensations flicked Martin. "What's not? You've said a lot, Sid."

". . . 'bout Angie."

"Sid — hold on."

A change edged over Trumbo's battered face. His head sagged.

Martin was gripping Trumbo's arm, thinking none of that mattered any more. Not any more. But after a moment he knew it did. It made a difference, too, because Sid had told him.

He could hear the distant rumble of the stampede when he mounted to bring the wagon. The buffalo would scatter and before long all would be hunted down, what the wolves didn't kill, down to the last forlorn old bull. And the wretched little band of Indians would be caught and returned to their miserable reservation.

But, he thought, that would be a while yet, and Sanford had his calves.

Nearing the wagons, he heard the pleasant hum of Harriet Sanford's calm voice. It held the promise of many things.